December 1994

for Elisa T
with love,
Mom

THE ANTI-EGOTIST

THE
ANTI–EGOTIST
KINGSLEY AMIS
MAN OF LETTERS

Paul Fussell

New York   Oxford

OXFORD UNIVERSITY PRESS

1994

Oxford University Press

Oxford   New York   Toronto
Delhi   Bombay   Calcutta   Madras   Karachi
Kuala Lumpur   Singapore   Hong Kong   Tokyo
Nairobi   Dar es Salaam   Cape Town
Melbourne   Auckland   Madrid

and associated companies in
Berlin   Ibadan

Copyright © 1994 by Paul Fussell

Published by Oxford University Press, Inc.,
200 Madison Avenue, New York, New York 10016

Oxford is a registered trademark of Oxford University Press

Library of Congress Cataloging-in-Publication Data
Fussell, Paul, 1924–
The anti-egotist : Kingsley Amis, man of letters / Paul Fussell.
p. cm.   Includes bibliographical references (p.) and index.
ISBN 0-19-508736-4
1. Amis, Kingsley.
2. Novelists, English—20th century—Biography.
3. Journalists—Great Britain—Biography.
I. Title. PR6001.M6Z65   1994
828'.91409—dc20   [B]   93-42010

1 3 5 7 9 8 6 4 2

Printed in the United States of America
on acid-free paper

To

SAMUEL WILSON FUSSELL

Preface

This book is about that part of Kingsley Amis's achievement which his highly successful novels have tended to overshadow. My focus is on his non-fiction and his literary learning, his performance as a critic, a learned anthologist, a memoirist, a teacher, and a poet—in short, a man of letters in the old sense, a writer conspicuous for complex literary knowledge and subtle taste as well as for vigorous views on politics and society.

His novels, after all, have generated lots of commentary, and readers can turn to such treatments as John McDermott's *Kingsley Amis: An English Moralist* (1989) and Dale Salwak's *Kingsley Amis, Modern Novelist* (1992). In this book I have not ignored the novels when they seem to bear on what I'm talking about, but I have attended largely to work that despite its excellence, in this age when *writer* seems virtually synonymous with *novelist,* has not attracted much critical attention.

I might note in passing that I have tried to exhibit and perhaps account for my devotion to British literary journalism and non-academic—decidedly non-academic—critical prose. I have always been delighted by what Richard Howard calls "discursive literature," things like biographies and autobiographies, travel books, war memoirs, and collections of literary essays and reviews. I'd rather re-read Cyril Connolly, Peter Quennell, and Orwell the essayist than all but a half-dozen of their novelist contemporaries. The book I'd most like to have written is Matthew Arnold's *Culture and Anarchy.*

In working from these premises I have had valuable help from Sir Kingsley, who kindly undertook to correct factual errors while leaving untouched all my opinions, no matter how exceptionable. I am happy to acknowledge help also from Edward T. Cone, Sam Fussell, John Gross, Lady Kilmarnock (Hilary), and Jack Lynch. I have relied on Dale Salwak's magisterial command of Amis bibliography, and I must thank George Justice for his conscientious and accurate research—and also for providing some well-written words which I have stolen. I am grateful to the Harry Ransom Humanities Research Center of the University of Texas for access to Amis's B. Litt. thesis, and I confess to recycling a bit I contributed to Salwak's *Kingsley Amis in Life and Letters* (1990). And again, to my wife Harriette, love and thanks.

Philadelphia   P. F.
July 1993

Contents

THE ANTI-EGOTIST

"Not a Very Nice Fellow"?

PA R T of the difficulty in seeing Amis as a figure of greater artistic and literary than polemic interest is his behavior during the Cold War. Then, nothing seemed to matter but a loud, uncompromising, and strenuous objection to everything that might be thought constructed after, or even recognizing, the Soviet model. Patriotism in both the United Kingdom and the USA he seemed to equate entirely with political conservatism, and he once suggested, perhaps not too seriously, that one of his women acquaintances who had ventured a left-wing enthusiasm was a member of the KGB. Usually an enemy of mere zeal, now he lost his cool.

The Cold War was thus hard on Amis, and it was perhaps harder on many of his former friends. His extravagantly expressed fear of Soviet tanks rolling west to install totalitarian governments all over Europe and finally in the British Isles drove him to rigidities of utterance which earlier he would have ridiculed as mechanical—and even totalitarian. He seemed to feel a need to foresee dangers to which less acute souls were willfully blind. Indeed, he took the presumed Russian military threat more seriously than many of the grandees of NATO itself. After the collapse of the Soviet satellites in Eastern Europe, after the dismantling of the Berlin Wall and the humiliating withdrawal of rusty Soviet armor with its hungry, abominably paid soldiers, I asked an American officer who had worked for years at NATO headquarters planning the tactical defense of the West how many high NATO officers actually believed the Russians would try to invade Western

Europe. "About one per cent," was his answer. But to Amis the threat was not political and dramatistic but real, and not just real but imminent. In this mind it was inextricably connected with the power-hunger of the Labour Party, the 1960s' expansion of the universities, the rise to intellectual respectability of the social sciences, and the worsening of London theater, literature, and civilized discourse in general.

Since most Americans with intellectual interests lean toward genteel forms of the political Left, Amis's American friends, many of them associated with universities, found themselves no longer treated by Amis as warmly as they once had been. Many dropped away entirely from friendship with a man who before the Cold War had seemed the quintessence of good sense, humor, tolerance, wit, and irony—irony about his own "positions" and views as well as others'. Friends were appalled to be confronted now with what appeared as literal-minded dogmatism and zeal. And not just on Eastern European matters but on most moral and political questions, now seen almost entirely from the political far Right. Kingsley had turned into Goldwater, Nixon, and General Westmoreland all at once, with sprinklings of William Buckley and R. Emmett Tyrrell, Jr. Where before the enemies had been social and literary pretentiousness and silliness, now also included was everyone leaning toward the Labour, Liberal, and in the USA, Democratic parties, and Britons friendly to Americanism, internationalism, the Common Market, the Maastricht Treaty, and the dilution of pure Anglo-Saxondom by immigration, especially non-Caucasian. Asked now if he's read a certain author, he might answer not with a reply but with a question: "He's a bit of a Lefty, isn't he?"

His catalog of dislikes broadened alarmingly, extending, many thought, to women, or at least the feminine character in general. Sometimes he was to be heard enunciating rules for men's and women's dress: the wearing by women of "peasant"-like garments (with sandals) he excoriated, as well as the wearing by men and boys of blazers displaying breast-pocket "coats of arms" worked in gold thread. Facial hair on males much below the age of seventy-five (Bernard Welch in *Lucky Jim* is an example) he interpreted as a warning of pomposity, ignorance, and probably leftiness to come. Walking sticks and tweed hats also became signals of offensiveness.

To some, his *Memoirs,* appearing in 1991, seemed to document these unattractive, Evelyn Waugh-like prejudices. In this book his outspoken and often rude, but always morally comic exposure of numerous phonies and pretenders to high culture (virtually unnoticed was his implicit celebration of modesty, taste, learning, and genuine, rather than publicized, literary achievement) seemed to solidify his reputation as a "literary rottweiler" whose only comfort now in his old age was to "nail and skewer, to lash and humiliate." *Guardian* writer Catherine Bennett also detected in his *Memoirs* "strains of misogyny, dissatisfaction, sentimentality, and vengefulness." (Although in a world like this, what's wrong, one must ask, with dissatisfaction?) In the USA the *Memoirs* encountered an even less subtle and discriminating audience. One bookseller in his catalog noted of Amis that "He didn't like anything," and Joel Conarroe, in a review in the *New York Times Book Review,* found Amis "not a very nice fellow," and his *Memoirs* simply "mischievous," largely a settling of old scores.

Conarroe's annoyance at Amis's comically exaggerated anti-Americanism—like many, he thinks American fiction and especially Saul Bellow gravely overrated—prevents his seeing why, after one dinner party, Amis satirizes the talented American creator of Hyman Kaplan, Leo Rosten. "There is no apparent reason on God's green earth for this essay," says Conarroe, "except to let the world know that [Amis] quickly lost patience with Rosten and his wife." But why? What is the reason "on God's green earth" that Conarroe doesn't see? What has offended Amis is what, as a moralist, always offends him, Rosten's affected, fake Europeanism and his American and caddish habit of self-praise. Rosten phones a nearby Italian restaurant for a reservation, and after a hearty and phony *"Buona sera!,"* with the headwaiter, expends all his show-Italian and subsides into English. At the table, Rosten explains what "Commencement" means at American schools and colleges, and proceeds to this:

> "Well, during the ceremony we get the Commencement Address, and the faculty . . . like to invite some kind of—"
> No single noun could come near doing justice to the mixture of self-deprecation, amusement, worldly wisdom, modesty, vanity and shittiness with which he spoke the next word.
> "—distinguished guy to deliver it."

And about his speech, Rosten reports, "the kids just *loved* it. They simply *exploded*. They *went wild*." And Conarroe still doesn't see how important it is to understand why Amis "lost patience with Rosten," or how this passage brings him into the company of Swift, Pope, Mark Twain, Flaubert, and H. L. Mencken. Moral satire is not common today, and only a few understand it. Amis is one of its best living practitioners, and it is depressing to see his attempts thrust aside as evidence merely of bad temper and irrational hatred. "Justice," says Aristotle, "consists in loving *and hating* aright." And in Amis's world, *aright* means on grounds which, although on the surface social, are underneath profoundly moral.

Amis has also given offense by his apparent misogyny, but in the works primarily complained of, *Jake's Thing* and *Stanley and the Women*, his satire is directed less at "women" than at the totalitarian strain in some kinds of theoretical feminism, as well as his favorite targets, egotism and affectation. A passage at the end of *Jake's Thing*, where Jake sums up his views on female faults, is often cited as evidence of Amis's convictions:

> Jake did a quick run-through of women in his mind, not of the ones he had known or dealt with in the past few months or years so much as all of them: their concern with the surface of things, with objects and appearances, with their surroundings and how they looked and sounded in them, with seeming to be better and to be right while getting everything wrong, their automatic assumption of the role of injured party in any clash of wills, their certainty that a view is more credible and useful for the fact that they hold it,

their use of misunderstanding and misrepresentation as weapons of debate, their selective sensitivity to tones of voice, their unawareness of the difference in themselves between sincerity and insincerity, their interest in importance (together with noticeable inability to discriminate in that sphere), their fondness for general conversation and directionless discussion, their pre-emption of the major share of feeling, their exaggerated estimate of their own plausibility, their never listening,

etc., etc. That seems better evidence of Jake's than Amis's misogyny, for the wild, conscious exaggeration (like Jake's *all of them*) will mislead no reader acquainted with classical satire or equipped with a sense of humor. Jake's decision to abjure sexual intercourse forever as a result of his string of examples should tip off the reader that this is supposed to be, in large part, funny. But just as there is some Jonathan Swift in the final proud, stiff Lemuel Gulliver, there's doubtless some Amis here as well, the Amis who is tired of the automatic imputation of virtue and special sensitivity to the female character. He is reacting against the twentieth-century's idealization of sex and marriage as well as against lingering Edwardian and Georgian rites of "chivalry," a body of beliefs and manners still dear to the upper classes. Women, Amis knows, can be fully as wicked as men. They can lie and cheat and destroy with the best of them, as they do in *Stanley and the Women* and *The Russian Girl.* Amis has encountered and thoroughly understood Lady Macbeth and Goneril, and reviewing Naim Attallah's book of interviews called *Women* (1987), he sees no reason to withhold his view that it is a showcase for "a bumper crop of raging egotists, pompous buffoons and unstoppable talkers, . . . with all humor and power of detachment virtually ruled out. To hear them go on, you would think that no female before them had ever been a child, got a job, met a man, had an affair, got married, had a baby or noticed that women are different from men and often have a different sort of life in certain respects."

So much for the misogyny charge, and so much for hating aright. But how about loving aright?

9

How does Amis come out there? One public form of love is social generosity, and this is one of Amis's obsessions, whether the focus is on decent "equal" treatment of defenseless social subordinates (waiters, maids, servants, drivers) and intellectual inferiors, or not stinting guests on drink or anything else, or making sure one's writing is accessible to ordinary people, likely to be put off by literary show-offs. Alun Weaver OBE, who has just returned to Wales after a successful London career as a Welsh broadcaster and Welsh authority and celebrity, is revealed in Amis's *The Old Devils* to be a triumph of egotism and phoniness, a vain popular-culture merchant and cliché purveyor whose lack of the literary talent he affects is betrayed not just by his inability to write anything sharp but by his total admiration of the works and behavior of the great modern Welsh poet-personality, "Bryden"—i.e., Dylan (Thomas). But worse is his cruelty to social inferiors whenever possible, and in front of a presumably admiring audience. Taking easy advantage is his social specialty, best illustrated in his end-of-lunch relations with a young local wine waiter in a modest Welsh town.

"What is the vintage port?" asks Alun, expecting to hear a date, and perhaps the name of a Portuguese shipper.

> "Port is a fortified wine from Portugal," said the waiter, having perhaps misheard slightly, "and vintage port is made from—"
> "I didn't ask for a bloody lecture on vinification, you horrible little man." Alun laughed a certain amount as he spoke. "Tell me the shipper and the year and then go back to your hole and pull the lid over it."
> The lad seemed more or less unabashed at this. "Graham 1975, sir," . . .

"It's no use just relying on respect to get good service in a restaurant," Alun explains to his tablemates. "There has to be fear too."

It is this sensitivity to daily cruelty that has made Amis, in his novels especially, one of the most conspicuous theorists of the malicious, the exercise of cruelty for its own sweet sake, as in the

Third Reich's treatment of the helpless or, in a dilute form, the easy recourse in all armies to humiliating the powerless. A while ago I told him something about my affection for many of the poems of the now unstylish Edmund Blunden, one of the most modest and kindhearted of English writers and thus also admired to some degree by Amis. I was rhapsodizing about Blunden's poem "Lonely Love," a reaction to the sight of a badly deformed couple devoted to each other:

> I love to see those loving and beloved
> Whom Nature seems to have spited; unattractive,
> Unnoticeable people, whose dry track
> No honey-drop of praise, or understanding,
> Or bare acknowledgment that they existed,
> Perhaps yet moistened. Still, they make their world.
>
> She with her arm in his—O Fate, be kind,
> Though late, be kind; let her have never cause
> To live outside her dream, nor unadore
> This underling in body, mind and type,
> Nor part from him what makes her dwarfish form
> Take grace and fortune, envy's antitone.
>
> I saw where through the plain a river and road
> Ran quietly, and asked no more event
> Than sun and rain and wind, and night and day,
> Two walking—from what cruel show escaped?
> Deformity, defect of mind their portion.
> But I forget the rest of that free day of mine,
> And in what flowerful coils, what airy music
> It led me here and on; these two I see
> Who, loving, walking slowly, saw not me,
> But shared with me the strangest happiness.

Discussing "Lonely Love" with Amis, I emphasized the line

> Deformity, defect of mind their portion,

and dwelt on the word *portion*, which I thought wonderfully evocative and memorable — resourceful, too, the way it gathers up seventeenth-century meanings of *destiny* and *God-allotted* social station. This use of *portion* triggered in Amis a memory dormant for many years, a memory capable of haunting for a lifetime one so sensitive to cruelty as he. Long ago he was observing an official female welfare worker addressing a needy man and woman who had asked to be vouchsafed some slight domestic item which might mitigate their misery a tiny bit. Declining snottily, she urged them not to forget their situation—irreversible destitution—and shrilled at them, with evident satisfaction, *"Want's* your portion!"* The man obsessed for decades with this little vignette of social cruelty may be thought at some distance from Conarroe's "not a very nice fellow," or at least much more complicated than the caricature Tory he is often taken for.

His concern with social generosity registers itself everywhere in his writings where meanness or stinginess is in evidence. In addition to satirizing Leo Rosten for egotism and self-satisfaction, Amis also has at him for niggardliness as a host. In Rosten's apartment before he phones in the exhibitionistic dinner reservation, Amis and wife are offered, as he recalls, exiguous Bloody Marys "about the size of a fairly large glass of sherry."

> We drank ours up rather fast and got another one of the same size. . . . [While Rosten was exhibiting his minimal Italian on the phone, his wife] noticed that Jane's and my glasses were again empty and, lowering her voice, asked us, "Would you like another drink?"
>
> She had not lowered it enough to escape the attention of Rosten, who slapped his hand across the telephone and said with some emphasis, "They've had two! They've had two!"

Finished with his phone call, Rosten relents, pouring his guests "a further diminutive drink before departure."

Amis's two-year stay at Peterhouse, Cambridge, as Director of Studies in English, was made more intolerable than even he expected by meanness with drink on the part of two Cambridge figures, the writer Andrew Sinclair and the scholar ("comparatist" he's been called in some places) George Steiner. Shortly after arriving in Cambridge, Amis received a note from Sinclair proposing a drink at his house. Although holding a low opinion of his writings—novels especially—Amis was willing, but when he phoned Sinclair to fix a time he was told, "Actually it's a bit awkward at the moment . . . We've got the builders in." Amis asked the Sinclairs to his place instead, and this first get-together was satisfactory enough "not to rule out another." Sinclair declared that it was their turn next time and that he'd phone soon.

When he rang he said, "I'm afraid we've still got the builders in."

I was ready for that. "We'll go to the pub," I said, and named my local. . . .

"This one's on me," said Sinclair firmly and unarguably as we moved towards the bar. "What will you have?" . . .

When the drinks came, Sinclair plunged his hand confidently into his top inner breast pocket. As in a dream I watched that confidence vanish in an instant, to be as quickly replaced by puzzlement, disbelief, consternation. Finally . . . "I must have left my wallet in my other jacket," he said.

Does Sinclair deserve the indictment? Was this a cunning evasion of an obligation? Probably not, merely an accident without much meaning, but to one so obsessed with generosity as Amis, even the accidental appearance of meanness can be taken as evidence of moral delinquency.

The case of George Steiner is a bit more complicated. There are many reasons why he puts Amis's back up. He's not just a Yank, but one so apparently ashamed to be one that he affects an elaborate European identity and writes pretentious pseudo-Continental intellectual works implying his command of virtually all European languages and literatures. In short, a phony. But as bad as Steiner's "cultural omniscience," Amis found, were the ungenerous "drinkless hiatuses at his dinner parties. After anything up to half an hour he would 'suddenly realize' his omission." (Amis has had some dissensions with Anthony Burgess, and one cause, in addition to the ones Amis specifies in the *Memoirs,* might be suggested by a blurb Burgess recently provided to publicize one of Steiner's public lectures: "My respect for Dr. Steiner as scholar, critic and novelist is as considerable as my admiration for him as a human being.") But on careful consideration, Steiner, in Amis's view, was overtaken by Sinclair, who "was reputed to offer his guests tea with the Chinese meal he was serving them, subtly finessing the 'wine of the country' principle."

Amis was at Cambridge in the early 1960s. Ten years later he published, in his small book *On Drink,* an ironic and comic chapter titled the "Mean Sod's Guide" to minimal drink service, refracting, one imagines, much of his experience with such as Sinclair and Steiner. In this hilarious chapter Amis's mode is close to Jonathan Swift's in his ironic *Directions to Servants,* but now, with servants only a dim memory, we have Amis's Directions to Hosts. "The point here," he begins, "is not simply to stint your guests on quality and quantity . . . but to screw them *while seeming, at any rate to their wives, to have done them rather well."* Both remoteness and delay can be exploited to minimize the number of pre-dinner drinks. These should be prepared "in some undiscoverable pantry or broom-cupboard well away from the main scene. This will not only screen your niggardlinesses; it will also make the fetching of each successive round look like a slight burden, and will cast an unfavorable limelight on any individual determined to wrest additional drinks out of you." Minimizing the outlay of wine at dinner requires a different technique. Here, you can husband your wine if you "suddenly remember" (like Steiner) that you've not yet brought it out. At any rate, you can get away with not serving it during the first course, and the opening of the bottle (hardly bottles) at the table can occasion a satisfactory delay. Stuffing guests with cheap carbohydrates during the first courses will save on the costly foods usually expected as entrees, and at the beginning, "a good ten minutes with no food in sight but rolls and butter will, as restaurants know, take the edge off most appetites."

Finally, the coffee-making should be public and ostentatious, so attention-demanding that serving drink at the same time can seem clearly impossible.

In the later twentieth century, with most other moral values in disarray, it would seem that meanness with drinks and food and other necessities is among the few remaining moral stigmas available for targeting by the satirist. Amis notes it widely and often, and sometimes in surprising forms, as when in *The Old Devils* he reveals that the Welshman Garth Pumphrey is content to risk broken limbs among his night-time guests rather than provide outdoor and porch light bulbs of anything but the lowest wattage. After his guests, invited for drinks, have stumbled into his dimly illumined house, they notice that "when everyone was indoors, Garth switched off the porch light, switched on a staircase light to indicate the lavatory on the landing, switched it off again and led them into a room at the back of the house." There, surveying thirstily the bottles ranged atop a sideboard, one guest observes something with "disquiet": the bottles are all equipped with the sort of measuring device found in bars and pubs to assure the exact pouring of a tot, no more. Regardless, the first round is served and enjoyed. But when refills are needed, it becomes clear that Garth expects normal pub procedure—that is, payment for goods received. "Just with the prices things are these days," Garth explains, "we simply can't afford unrestricted hospitality. Of course we'd like to, but we can't." When Garth now has recourse to a pocket calculator, some readers may think the comedy a bit too broad. Others may not. Alun Weaver, up to his old trick of embarrassing anyone handy, adjures Garth not to forget, in his calculations, the cost of the first round of drinks. Garth, offended, comes alight: "Those first drinks were not a *round* in any sense of the word. They were my freely offered hospitality. Good God, man, do you take me for some kind of Scrooge?" A memorable contrast to Garth in Amis's fiction might be Gore-Urquhart, in *Lucky Jim*, who, to calm Jim's nerves before his crucial lecture, produces "a slim but substantial flask" and provides Jim with not just one but two slugs. For all the comedy, and despite the necessity of Gore-Urquhart as a plot mechanism, he stands as Amis's type of the traditional magnanimous man, implicit as a hero in all Amis's writings.

Charging your guests for drinks is just one of the ways you can reveal your meanness. Another is visible stinginess about razor blades and haircuts. In *Lucky Jim,* Johns appears one morning at the communal boarding-house breakfast table with his "lard-like pallor . . . diversified by several inflamed patches (the consequence, no doubt, of shaving with a blade far too blunt for anybody with a normal attitude towards money). . . ." In addition, his hair looks funny, the result, it transpires, of his operating on his own hair with a pair of clippers. "Too sodding mean to pay out his one-and-six," comments Beesley. The same behaviour characterizes the stooge landlord Dick Thompson in *Take a Girl Like You.* He does with cigarettes what the normal drink-round evader does with pub drinks. At one point Patrick says, "He didn't offer his cigarettes round once last night. Not once. I watched particularly." Another time, Dick is seen secretly repairing a tear in one of his cigarettes with a bit of gummed paper. Of course he buys the cheapest toilet paper for his residents and turns out all possible lights—even of the lowest power—making his stairways a notable hazard. Amis observed signs of a regrettable closeness even in his friend Philip Larkin, and even there he can't help seeing stinginess as evidence of a more profound liability, "emotional parsimony," manifested in Larkin's apparent disinclination to run the risk of wife and children, to essay the hazards of domestic life like others of his age and education. Amis, who loved and admired Larkin perhaps more than any of his other friends, told John Mortimer: "He was unlike us. He never threw himself at life. Marriage, adultery, all that sort of thing. He avoided all that."

For all the sometimes rowdy comedy attending Amis's depictions of meanness, his understanding of its psychology is complicated and serious. It is, if funny, also immoral, so little and minimal, practiced by wee men only. And it betrays neurosis, implying constant "paranoid" watchfulness lest one be had. It keeps one on a constant stretch of attentive calculation, and this finally becomes a substitute for thought, as well as replacing an objective interest in things outside oneself. In writers, for Amis selfishness results in a willed obscurity that withholds the generous participation of meaning with a reader. Meanness becomes something like a metaphor for all sorts of artistic perversions, and even in Amis's criticism of restaurants, the theme is never far from the surface. In praising Lane's Restaurant in the *Illustrated London News,* for example, he notes that its generosity, "providing more than the minimum," is a signal of imagination at work—identification with the thoughts and hopes of others.

For Amis generosity is not just a literary or abstract value. One Christmas, he loaded my young son with wonderful costly gifts, including his first typewriter, because he wanted to augment his self-respect and make him happy. And once during a lunch party at a restaurant in Wales, at which he was the host, he was so struck by the intelligence, charm, generosity, and humor of the local waitress that at the end he closed her hand around an extravagant tip, amounting to about fifty dollars, enough for her to buy, say, a new dress. For him, generosity is not just a static psychological and ethical condition of the personality, a mere disposition to do good. It must be constantly renewed in action. In his story "Dear Illusion" the narrator says, "Worry about others' concerns, like pleasure on their account, needs regular renewal if it is not to fall away." The waitress provided an opportunity for a renewal, but such opportunities confront Amis constantly in his work as critic, editor, and commentator.

Consider the motif of generosity lurking in his comments on poems in his anthologies. In *The Pleasure of Poetry,* aimed at the good-hearted but not necessarily literary reader, he notes of the hero of Newbolt's Victorian classic "Vitaï Lampada" ("Play up, play up and play the game"), that his pre-eminent virtue is unselfishness, where others might be struck by such conspicuous military virtues as bravery, persistence, or self-sacrifice. And in this same anthology, commenting on Isaac Watts's hymn "Our God,

Our Help in Ages Past," he goes out of his way to inform the common reader about something that has nothing to do with anything in the hymn—namely, that Watts "was a charitable man who for many years gave a third of his limited income to the poor." With that, it's hard to forget Samuel Johnson's explanation of his reason for including Watts, despite his minor literary status, in his *Lives of the Poets:* "I wish to distinguish Watts, a man who never wrote but for a good purpose."

Student

SIR Kingsley Amis grew up in an unprepossessing two-up, two-down semi-detached in the dreary southwest London suburb of Norbury, near Croydon, an unprivileged, unbeautiful, and boring place. He was an only child of middle-class parents. His father, "the most English human being I have ever known," went to work in the City immediately after graduating from the City of London School and worked all his life as a clerk for Colman's Mustard, "the horrible mustard people," Amis calls them.

His *Memoirs* encountered severe criticism from some readers failing to recognize the moralist's and satirist's way he dealt with some of his now defunct relatives. Of his paternal grandfather, "Dadda," he noted "how much I disliked and was repelled by him." Dadda's wife he depicts as a model of stinginess, who left the maids only two matches for lighting the gas in the morning, who eked out the supply of toilet paper with cut up bits of old paper bags, and who seemed to entertain as little as possible, lest she spend money. She was "a large dreadful hairy-faced creature who lived to be nearly ninety and whom I loathed and feared in a way I had never felt towards Dadda." He had better luck with one of his mother's parents, her father being relatively civilized, a reader and book collector, whose library contained numerous volumes of good poetry (Wordsworth, Coleridge, Byron, Keats, Shelley). But his wife, "Gran," hated literature and became for the young Amis a caricature of the viciously destructive philistine. "He would read his favorite passages aloud to her and she would make

21

faces and gestures at him while his head was lowered to the page, which helped to make me hate her very much."

Amis's mother's young sister Dora was a character of a different sort, a clinically anxious neurotic wearing "a permanently disaffected expression." From her behavior the child Amis quickly gathered that she was, if harmlessly, "off her head." This perception, he notes, "can have done little to alleviate the fears of madness which have worried me from time to time throughout my life." Dora had once been a moderately successful professional singer, but as she aged her eccentricities grew upon her and she was finally received into a mental institution, where she flourished. No wonder a child so intelligent and sensitive, growing up among these oddities, "was always nervous. Full of fear." Indeed, he says, "I was afraid someone would come into my bedroom and murder me." Despite occasional acts of public bravado, Amis's shyness and vulnerability persist, and it may be suspected that his friendliness towards drink is in part due to its usefulness as social lubrication and insulation. In *On Drink* he refers to liquor's function in social ice-breaking, in easing the trauma of "a sudden confrontation with complete or comparative strangers in circumstances requiring a show of relaxation and amiability—an experience that I, for one, never look forward to without misgiving, even though I nearly always turn out to enjoy it in the event."

Neither of his parents was religious, and he is a bit aggrieved that they provided no access to religious instruction—or musical instruction either: he still regrets his inability to play the piano. But his father did not stint instruction in another subject, sex, warning him about the dire consequences of masturbation, which at first "thinned the blood" and ultimately and inevitably propelled its practitioners to madhouses, where they could be seen furiously wanking all the time. But father did him an unwitting favor by stimulating him to violent argument frequently and thus helping to refine the boy's polemic skills. As Amis says, "We quarrelled violently at least every week or two for years." Both were extremely stubborn, and father wanted son to become an all-but exact version of himself. For his part, the young Amis had acquired, as he now reports, "a very liberal helping of adolescent intellectual's arrogance, while inheriting in full measure my father's obstinacy." One occasion of loud and abusive disagreement was the topic of high-popular versus highbrow taste in music. Father was ecstatic over Gilbert and Sullivan, but when taken by his father to *The Pirates of Penzance* or *The Yeomen of the Guard,* Kingsley cruelly overplayed his boredom. Young Amis wanted, he said, Schubert, Haydn, Brahms, together with such un-English imports as Benny Goodman and Duke Ellington. The thin walls of the Amis residence made it impossible to screen from father's hearing these exotic sounds conveyed from the BBC into the family's wireless. Furious arguments were inevitable and constant.

Kingsley's preference for reading over "family conversation" was another source of trouble with father, and sometimes with mother as well. Anything suggesting the value of intellectual privacy, if not secrecy, struck them as slightly sinister. It was made clear to this already intense young scholar that "reading in public was deemed rude, while reading in private was deemed anti-social." What was demanded was the loathed experience of "joining in the family circle." Kingsley also disappointed father by his want of skill in cricket, a game father played with distinction. In sum, boredom, Amis asserts, was his main response to his father's presence, and the boredom increased with his aging parent's bent towards irrelevant anecdotal narrative late in life. The mature Amis now recognizes that his father must have been equally bored by his accounts of university and army life and the like, and he is led, now, to this conclusion: "It is depressing to think how persistently dull and egotistical we can be to those we most value, and how restless and peevish we get when they do it back to us." But it's hard to do much about this terrible fact, he observes, "given the burning sincerity of all boredom."

His mother influenced him in two profound ways: by setting an example as an inveterate reader, not, to be sure, of the greatest stuff but of books all the same; and by, for whatever reason, not having another child, so that Kingsley was forced upon himself and his own resources without the dissipation of focus that play or fights or idling with siblings might have produced. That is, very early he learned to concentrate and to blot out all distraction, an indispensable requirement for the development of the literary character. Perhaps he didn't fully realize what had been missing from his childhood until a quarter-century later, when during his first trip to the USA he visited his aunt and uncle in Washington: "It was a small house and not a prosperous household. . . . But they had their sun-porch and the rumpus room and plenty of parties, and in a beat-up-Chevvy, hamburger-joint kind of way they showed us something very American: what a good time non-well-off people could have." What was missing in Amis's early environment was, in short, joy, the capacity for it, the demand for it, and the expectation of it.

The boy Amis was first sent to a nearby school, where he was lonely and miserable and where another boy duly bit his arm, but where he at least had his initial brush with English literature at the hands of the curiously elegant Miss Barr. His next school was the now vanished Norbury College, and this was more like it—or maybe Kingsley was now old enough to know how to wring from a school what he needed and to benefit from the teachers who appealed to him. One master got him interested in algebra, another in reading adventure stories. But the best was Mr. Ashley, who inducted his pupils into the delights of poetry, even modern (that is, mostly Georgian) poetry, who made them write essays on non-utilitarian topics, and who even made them try writing poetry in assigned stanzaic and metrical forms.

Next, Amis was enrolled in the City of London School, where he quickly learned that one key to popularity was a talent to amuse. He refined his art of mimicry—especially of the headmaster—and thus ingratiated himself with his fellow wits. At City of London he was fortunate to be deeply influenced by a gifted teacher of English, the Reverend C. J. Ellingham, who augmented his instruction with unsuperficial side-glances at the history of art and music.

Ellingham was a visible and sincere Christian, but in his announced fondness for the poems of Housman, including the most skeptical and even blasphemous ones, he conveyed a lesson Amis has never forgotten: "I saw for ever that a poem is not a statement and the poet 'affirmeth nothing'."

At City of London, Amis cut sports whenever possible, sensing accurately that he was not that type, but he did enroll in the Officers' Training Corps, where he found that he rather enjoyed close-order drill (he was a cadet sergeant and got to give the commands). He also found that he was an excellent shot with a rifle. Military imagery so seized his mind that "for quite some time I thought that if I failed to become a writer I would go into the army." And from schooldays to this, the army has been a strong presence in Amis's consciousness, both as an emblem of fatuity and, conversely, as a source of invaluable heroic standards. Like life: absurd, but also serious.

In the summer of 1939, with the bombing of London correctly forecast, the school was evacuated to Wiltshire, to be attached to the elite and, in Amis's eyes, grossly snobbish Marlborough College. During the five terms he was at Marlborough, no social overtures were made towards the City of London boys, the Marlborough students remaining "entirely aloof." The brighter boys were preparing for university, and Amis now wanted to change his concentration from Classics to English. This required a great deal of adjustment and trouble and extra work, but the result was a scholarship in English at St. John's College, Oxford. Amis remains grateful to the City of London School. "I have never in my life," he says, "known a community where factions of any kind were less in evidence, where differences of class, upbringing, income group and religion counted for so little. . . . The academic teaching was of a standard not easily to be surpassed, but more important still was that lesson about how to regard one's fellows, a lesson not delivered but enacted."

He entered Oxford in April, 1941. It was not the best time to embark on a career associated with liberal learning and contemplation. The dreaming spires were intact, but little else was. In North Africa, Rommel was driving the British back after seizing Benghazi. The Germans were bombing Belgrade, killing 17,000 civilians there. Closer to home, aircraft factories near Coventry were bombed, and on April 12, Churchill and the American ambassador Gilbert Winant toured Bristol to raise morale after the savage bombing of the city center. A few days later twenty-two civilian hostages were murdered in Paris for the shooting of a German corporal in the Métro. And even at Oxford it was clearly wartime. The pre-war party scene had closed down entirely, what with severe shortages of liquor, clothing, cigarettes, and fuel. Amis was poor too. On arrival, he was introduced to sherry. As a beginner, he drank too much and was sick. After that, he tended to stick to beer. His idealistic understanding of the meaning of fairness, as well as his hatred of social snobbery reinforced by his experiences at Marlborough, attracted him to the student branch of the Communist Party, where he met girls, tried to read Marx and Lenin, attended "study groups," and learned at first hand "the unquenchable assiduity with which Communists infiltrate other groups. . . ."

Already familiar with junior military usages from the City of London OTC, Amis also joined the Oxford Senior Training Corps, and again excelled in close-order drill, which was about all the unit seemed to do. Soon Amis met Larkin, who signalled goodwill immediately by offering a cigarette. It was wit, sensitivity, intelligence, and American jazz that cemented their long friendship.

From 1942 to 1945 Amis was in the army, but he resumed his Oxford career in the autumn of 1945. Deprivation had made him avid for women and drink, but now study began to seem attractive too. He found that the language and literature of Old and Middle English, then an indispensable part of the required literature curriculum, bored, horrified, and depressed him. (Since then, he says, he's rather changed his mind, having perceived that post-Chaucerian writing, to which he turned with relief as soon as possible, should probably not be taught in universities at all but left for the curious to discover on their own for entertainment and illumination.) He liked Spenser and of course Shakespeare, but found Donne an early example of the stylistic show-off, more concerned to exhibit his own cleverness than to convey delightful meaning to the reader. Amis finally won his First-Class degree, but to do so he had to commit terrible lies in the obligatory Old English paper. "I have never written anything finer in its way [than an excursus on a primitive poem in Old English] . . . a positive firework-display of hypocrisy and affectation."

Aware now that university lecturing would doubtless be his destiny, for the sake of job safety he decided in 1948 to go for the next degree, a B. Litt., at the same time courting and marrying Hilary (Hilly) Bardwell and moving with her into quarters in the Oxford suburbs. The B. Litt. required a thesis registering the results of original research or understanding. Amis chose to work on Victorian poetry and its audiences. (Noting that very few people read poetry, he was naturally curious about what it was like when a lot of people did and when new poems by heavyweight Victorians constituted news.) He was allotted the Oxford don Lord David Cecil as his thesis supervisor. Cecil was an Oxford curiosity—effeminate (although vividly heterosexual), flamboyant, notably lazy, a popular, if flabby and often incoherent lecturer. All this set off by a ridiculous hat and an affected voice hard to distinguish from a "nanny-goat squeal." A pronounced lisp completed the ensemble. Amis soon found that Cecil was too idle to interest himself in supervisory duties, and after much frustration, he sought out the more responsive F. W. Bateson, who agreed to displace Cecil. It was only, thought Amis, a matter of getting Cecil to sign a form. He did so, but apparently did not forget or forgive the implicit suggestion that he had somehow fallen short, and that a colleague knew it.

Now teaching at the University College of Swansea, Amis struggled away at the thesis and finally returned to Oxford for his oral examination. Horror! Lord David was one of the two examiners, the other being a junior easily cowed. Cecil contrived to flunk Amis. But because he already had his Assistant Lectureship at Swansea, the failure didn't matter except as a sign of wasted time and effort. The whole experience, actually, was far from a waste, for the reading and thinking the thesis required familiarized Amis with important poems and emphasized for him some crucial determinants on the way literature is produced, received, and preserved. And his immersion in Victorian literary practices established firmly in his mind, at the very outset of his career, that literature should not consist of the by-products of auctorial self-indulgence and self-amusement but should rather be a responsible social transaction with readers, who must be treated with the normal courtesy governing civilized social occasions. In writing, this means clarity, leading to pleasurable enlightenment. The term *writer* has today become an honorific loosely used. Amis would probably not object if the term were restricted to people who have readers. The spoiling of reams of paper without that crucial criterion makes one not a writer but a vandal, or a failed exhibitionist.

The somewhat stiff academic title of Amis's 156-page thesis was *English Non-Dramatic Poetry, 1850–1900, and the Victorian Reading Public.* In it, he considers the relation to their readers, when the reading of new poetry was intellectually inviting and socially almost obligatory, of Dante Gabriel Rossetti, George Meredith, Christina Rossetti, William Morris, James Thomson, Swinburne, Gerard Manley Hopkins, Wilde, Edward Fitzgerald, and Tennyson and Browning. It was a highly ambitious project requiring deep research in Victorian periodicals, biographies, correspondences, commentaries, and memoirs. It took solid labor, and although today Amis seems to brush it off as a slightly absurd boyish academic exercise, it is a valuable work. Its general excellence would fulfill high academic requirements almost everywhere and its solidity suggests that Cecil's reaction was in the main more spiteful than responsible.

Amis begins by emphasizing that "Like all other artistic endeavors, the writing of poetry is a social act. . . ." Then, at the beginning of the second paragraph, a sentence that gave Lord David his first opportunity to object: "A poet writes his poetry originally for a small circle of intimate friends, keeping before him as he writes their probable response, and afterwards soliciting their opinion." In the margin here Lord David scrawled "Always?"; and in the oral examination he asked aggressively, "Alwayth?" Amis tried to indicate that he knew his point was a generalization with some exceptions, but Lord David, perhaps sensing a threat to his own romantic conception of the way poetry flows out magically and without calculation, was relentless after this. As the thesis continues, his question marks appear singly and in multiples in Amis's margins. Statements like the following are sure to activate Cecil's pencil: When a poet ceases "to write for his inner audience, his work, as well as his fame, will suffer." To a romantic critic, there's dangerous aesthetic skepticism there. (It's no surprise to find that at Swansea, Amis was giving a course touching on eighteenth-century literary criticism.)

This *inner audience* is the first of the poet's three audiences. Next, there is the *intermediate audience,* whom many might want to designate *fans.* These are readers excited by the poet's publications, constituting "a band of followers who owe allegiance primarily to him rather than to other poets." That is, in modern terms, readers who read everything Auden, say, publishes, and who in their devotion to his work wouldn't waste time reading, say, Stephen Spender or C. Day Lewis. This intermediate audience tends to be sectarian and quite snobbish, "conscious that it values what is not generally valued." When its work of enthusiastic possession and recommendation is over, and "its hero the property of the many, its enthusiasm largely subsides." The public enthusiasm of this intermediate audience, manifested in reviews, bookshop demand, and general literary agitation, stimulates the curiosity of the third group of readers, the *outer audience,* consisting of people vulnerable to publicity and fashion. This three-part analysis of audiences is, to be sure, too heavy and unwieldy to explain much. It is a "system," surely original, but not, in the end, terribly useful, and most valuable, perhaps, as a gesture towards demystifying and desentimentalizing the literary process and thus giving useful offense to the shallow, the thoughtless, and the genteel. Whatever its value, this analysis of literary audiences represents Amis's uncomfortable attempt to do something learned and almost "scientific" with a humane subject resistant to such procedures.

His discomfort can be gauged by the academic clichés he apparently felt appropriate as he began his exposition. Anyone hoping to describe Amis's mature prose style might begin by saying that it is the exact reverse of his thesis idiom, with its pompous bromides, its reliance on the passive voice, its frequent elaborate periphrasis: "The student . . . has every reason to be grateful," he writes. "The evidence assembled in the previous paragraph necessitates the conclusion that—." It is "a matter for some regret." "There has also been offered some ground for speculation that—," and so on. This suggests that Amis could not write as long as he was obliged to take seriously the academic milieu and the sort of readers it tended to spawn. These horrible examples, it must be said, all come from the early part of the thesis. Clumsy and inauthentic locutions tend to vanish utterly once Amis gets into the job of talking about something real, the poets, their poems, and what people thought of them.

As he proceeds, he implicitly projects his Victorian poets as models of literary behavior for all times and places, socially generous enough to consider always the rights of the audience to be addressed with minimal obscurity and egotism. Poor Hopkins, thus: his inner audience consisted almost wholly of the bemused Robert Bridges, who, with his interest in literary theory and critical abstractions and warmed-over Platonism, not to mention the finer points of prosody, was, Amis observes, "poorly equipped to serve Hopkins as an inner audience." Oscar Wilde and similar Decadents and Aesthetes are specified as monitory examples, having produced "poetry that is among the most faded of any written in the nineteenth century." The trouble with the Aesthetic position is, ultimately, snobbery, a conviction that "communication is not a necessary part of the literary process." There in essence are the solid reasons for Amis's later apparently merely reactionary rejection of Pound and Picasso and Stravinsky. Regardless of his public "politics," Amis actually displays all the marks of a cultural democrat. Like Samuel Johnson, he is always on the side of the "common reader" against the don, the pedant, the specialist, the theorist, and the hobbyist, against, indeed, all who would use literature and art largely as a means for exhibiting their own acuteness or superiority. But in stressing the necessity of communication in poetry, Amis draws back from a total egalitarianism, which merely invites new forms of snobbery and exclusivism, like social primitivism, with its reduction of "poetry" to pub performances of forgettable free verse to guitar accompaniment. Considering with some disappointment Tennyson's late, highly popular career, Amis observes bravely, "It seems logical that a poet should write for his readers, but dangerous if he writes for readers who are also his intellectual inferiors."

This desire for excessive popularity is one threat to poetry. Another is equally social and moral, as illustrated by George Meredith's incompetence in social relations, reflecting his will to dominate and his lack of interest in others. "His conversation," Amis notes, "tended to monologue and didacticism, and with his children and social inferiors, to jocular offensiveness." (Here, the hand of a reader, probably Lord David, has scrawled a question mark in the margin.) Meredith insisted on his privacy, a posture clearly at some odds with the implications of the word *publication.* And his angry determination to keep it all to himself cost him dearly. He had (in Amis's terms) no inner audience; his intermediate audience was slow to develop and not large; and his outer audience has been minimal. All this not because he was a bad writer but because of his personal and social defects. From this sad case Amis concludes: "If writing is a social gesture, it might be possible to trace a correlation between a man's attitude to his writing and his general social attitude." Amis himself is of course a prime illustration of precisely that correlation.

William Morris is another author, Amis finds, damaged by his moral and social defects. He did manage to assemble an inner audience, to whom he read his drafts, but his motive was less a desire to communicate and to receive criticism than simple vanity. Self-love weakened his writing because he declined to slow down his profuse production. As Amis writes, "Morris . . . sacrificed the task of communication, with its inevitable self-criticisms, irritations and ponderings . . . to the easier pleasure of putting words down," and doing so twelve hours a day. Although Amis admires Swinburne for memorizing and reciting his new poems when he set them before his inner audience, his social isolation kept him from a continuous knowledge of other people, with the result that he lost the power to judge what would affect readers. Here Amis cites with enthusiasm the words of T. Earle Welby's *A Study of Swinburne* (1926) about Swinburne's decline as a poet:

> It is the curse of solitude that one's ideas and emotions, no longer having to be apprehended with the utmost nicety for conveyance to others, tend to become vague.

(A good reason, among others, for the habit of moderate social drinking, which willy nilly requires contact with others.)

If Amis has a hero in his thesis, it is Dante Gabriel Rossetti, in part because of "his unexpected insistence on entertainment as an essential quality of poetry." Rossetti once declared, "Good poetry is bound to be *amusing,*" without at all intending to imply that it should be funny: he meant engaging, un-boring regardless of the seriousness of the subject, written so as to pass what Amis calls "the night-owl test: When everyone else has gone to bed, how many poets compete successfully with a new recording of the Tchaikovsky B flat minor . . . ? In my case, the answer to this question (a more serious and searching one than anything involving hierarchies of merit) is—remarkably few: Housman, parts of Graves, Betjeman, the early Tennyson, the Macaulay of 'Horatius,' the early R. S. Thomas, and Philip Larkin." This night-owl test, one may observe in passing, is a typically Amisian invitation to absolute intellectual honesty in criticism. There's no better test of one's own honesty, as well as the power of a given poem to survive, than to choose to read it when no one is looking. Such honesty with oneself Rossetti recognizes as indispensable in the production of art worth having. One can't address the reader effectively without addressing oneself honestly, and thus Rossetti emphasizes "that self-examination and self-confronting with the reader which are in an absolutely unwearied degree necessary in art." Numerous writers of imaginative works have toiled to imagine themselves into the bodies and minds of their characters, some very distant in attributes from themselves, but how many have undergone such strenuous efforts of identification and understanding with another character, the reader? Rossetti again:

> Above all ideal personalities with which the poet must learn to identify himself, there is one supremely real which is the most imperative of all; namely, that of his reader. And the practical watchfulness needed for such assimilation is as much a gift and an instinct as is the creative grasp of alien character.

And Rossetti goes on to emphasize the quasi-mystical, almost religious nature of this exercise in democratic fellow-feeling: "It is a spiritual contact . . . which must be a part of the very act of production." In short, you can't fake it or add it afterwards.

Amis's B. Litt. thesis, academic sketchbook though it may be, resonates with autobiographical implications. In his *Memoirs* he quotes Anthony Powell's saying, "In vino veritas—I don't know, but in scribendo veritas—a certainty." The undeclared burden of the thesis is a shy, uncertain writer's hope for support among his friends. Growing more and more comfortable writing for this familiar audience, the writer will come to regard his distant audience as familiar and friendly too, and thus he can address it with security. It's like social drinking in a way, a matter of comfort and ease. Some members of Amis's inner audience are gone now: Larkin, George Gale, his physician friend John Allison, Tibor Szamuely, John Betjeman. Robert Conquest remains, and so does

Anthony Powell. And Martin Amis has been enlisted as a worthy replacement. Even so diminished an inner audience will help suggest the character of the intermediate and outer audiences Amis writes for. "A writer's audience is and remains invisible to him," he says, "but if he is any good he is acutely and continuously aware of it."

Soldier

FAMILY, school, and university are of course places where you learn, but as with many of his generation much of Amis's education and preparation for understanding and for literature he owes to the army. "One of the things the army does for you," he says, "is to enlarge your concept of human nature and of what is possible." One thing taught by that strictly hierarchical environment, lavish with punishments and humiliations, is how cruel human beings can be to each other. I don't mean shooting prisoners or tormenting the enemy wounded for the fun of it. Amis was in the Royal Corps of Signals, a technical, non-bellicose branch of the army, and he saw little of that sort of physical cruelty. But what he did see was almost as stomach-turning, and he didn't have to go all the way to wartime Normandy and Belgium to see it.

Once, at a unit dance, he witnessed a scene almost too bold for fiction. Present were the Adjutant, his wife, and six or seven others, and drinks had been circulating freely. Almost fifty years later Amis's recall of the scene in his *Memoirs* is vivid:

> "I've told her often enough," the Adjutant was saying. "It's not my fault there isn't any kid after nearly ten years. I'm doing my part when the time comes round. It's her who's not doing hers. Must be."
>
> "I think we could go into this another time, Ted," said his friend.
>
> "I'm not having her sitting there and saying that's right, we

37

haven't got a kid but nobody seems to know why," said the Adjutant. "It's *her fault* and that's an end of it. *I* can manage what the book says you have to do. *She's* the one who unfortunately can't perform the necessary. Everybody got that?"

His wife, with her hands over her face, had certainly got that. Why she was still sitting there I could not imagine. Nor could I think of anything anybody could have done. Ticking a man off for maltreating his wife in public is notoriously delicate, especially, if the man is senior among a group of officers.

"*Barren.* That's what it used to be called. . . ."

I forget what happened after that. I think I was overtaken by one of those horrible moments of suspicion apt to strike a young man at such times, that what he had just seen is a sample of what life, grown-up life in the real world of earning a living and having a family, is actually like, and that what he has tried to believe up to now has been based on reading too much poetry, etc.

Amis's abundant experience of such shits in the army provided impetus for the numerous examples in his novels, people like Roger Micheldene in *One Fat Englishman,* Bernard Bastable in *Ending Up,* and of course Alun Weaver in *The Old Devils.*

Soon Amis was a boy lieutenant whose section of about forty men handled telephone, telegraph, and messenger communications for the HQ of the British Second Army. This required constant attentiveness and earned frequent automatic reprimands from above, the standard experience of junior officers. The photograph of himself with his section in his *Memoirs* is touching and interesting. Looking like a choirboy, Lieutenant Amis stands in the front row next to a notably taller, and tougher, sergeant. With a few exceptions, the rest of the men, although many were skilled telegraphers who had been post-office employees, radio and electrical technicians and the like, look by contrast as if recruited from boxing rings or coal mines. Amis is clearly not like these others, and actually he sometimes got into trouble by being polite and decent to them, giving the impression of deficiency in the firmness and snottiness appropriate to "command."

Like most men who were young and healthy in the 1940s and spent several years in the service, Amis has been indelibly marked by it. It's true that even without this experience he might have developed his fondness for "military" poems like those of Macaulay, Southey, Browning, Kipling, and Housman, but it's doubtful that he would have conceived an affection for a character type seldom encountered outside the army, the long-service senior noncommissioned officer, skilled in managing his superiors without giving punishable offense, adept at securing and safeguarding items, especially liquids, not strictly lawful or appropriate, and proficient in his own brand of straightfaced comic irony. For example: after the war, in Germany, Amis and a senior sergeant watch a beautiful girl the no-fraternization rule forbids their having to do with. The sergeant to Amis: "I'd rather sleep with her with no clothes on than you in your best suit, sir." A "semantic somersault" is the way Amis describes that sort of thing. Another variety of senior NCO talk could be designated unpunishable ironic insolence: "Are you waiting to see me, sergeant-major?" "No, sir, I'm just standing here for a bet." Like "cheap at half the price," another army favorite, these are, says Amis, "surviving examples of what must in the past have been a huge stock pervading army life and other parts of 'low' life, now surely all forgotten. There would have been one or more for every detail or moment of a soldier's day, concretizing it, ironizing it." These folk witticisms were the property of people seldom met by the bookish or the educated. They belonged to the highly intelligent but unschooled, a class Amis, the cultural democrat, has never forgotten or lost his admiration for, a class he knows, when at universities, is always out there beyond the walls, often providing more insight and amusement than many installed safely within the academy.

Amis is so fond of the long-service Other Rank as a type of cunning and survival that he's often emplaced examples in his fiction. In the short story "I Spy Strangers," there is Sergeant Doll, efficient, cynical, profoundly and accurately critical of the pretensions to adequacy of most of his officers, especially the unit commander, Major Raleigh. In one frank postwar talk with junior officer Archer, Sgt. Doll descants on the Major:

> It may surprise you to learn that I can't think of anybody whom I despise as thoroughly as I despise the major. . . . He's so sure he's better. But in fact he's shoddy material. Third rate. Not to be depended on. . . . He's soft. He'll break. . . . No principle.

Another old NCO is ex-company-sergeant-major Furze, in *The Egyptologists*, once the platoon sergeant of one of the members. He now serves as the club's steward, overseeing the liquor supply and delivering sardonic Other Ranks' observations like "Sex is playing with yourself in company." Most of the members are ex-officers, and Furze takes it for granted that one of his duties is to keep them up to snuff. Of one member proving soft in a crisis—the real purpose of the society is to provide an alibi for members spending evenings with women not their wives—Furze notes: "He's the sort to go to pieces under fire." Furze imposes a quasi-military style on all his relations with the members, and when he wishes to address them almost as an equal, he warns that he's going to speak "very much off parade." The third member of this triumvirate is Derrick Shortell, in *Ending Up.* Known as Shorty, he is a retired company quartermaster-sergeant and onetime boyfriend of cashiered ex-officer Bernard Bastable, one of the superannuated residents of Tuppenny-hapenny Cottage. His years of clandestine trade in army supplies have honed his ingenuity, and he is skilled at concealing in various hiding places the bottles of booze on which he relies to get through the day. He exemplifies, says Amis, "that strange, insepa-rable mixture of real, almost instinctive obedience, and covert, largely futile disobedience which long Army service in the ranks so often creates." Actually, these old NCOs come close to constitut-ing the heroes of the works in which they appear. If their wisdom is cynical, it is still wisdom, based on decades of shrewd and accurate observation of actual, not theoretical, human behavior. They have now in common the ability to make no mistakes. They don't get things wrong, ever. Their understanding of situations is always the one proved correct by events. Their view of human nature has been thoroughly earned, and Amis respects it deeply, while at the same time enjoying them as comic characters.

During his spell in the army Amis kept his eyes fully open, and his later recall of the military atmosphere is acute and detailed. In addition to "I Spy Strangers," two more stories register among other things the moral pressures experienced by junior officers. In "My Enemy's Enemy," the question is, how loyal must a young man be to his officer colleagues, especially those he dislikes or scorns? And in "Court of Inquiry," the question is, how much lying is justified to get oneself out of a predicament inherently ridiculous but which must be taken as if seriously? There is even more army in *The Anti-Death League,* a novel revealing an almost uncanny mastery of military atmosphere and details.

Amis is no uncritical admirer of Norman Mailer, another writer whose view of life was in large part determined by his early encounter with it in rigorous institutional form, the army. Indeed, it seems hard for Amis to mention Mailer at all without getting in a moralist's jab about Mailer's once stabbing his wife in a fury. But Amis does admire two of Mailer's fictions, *The Naked and the Dead* and the short story "The Language of Men." Both explore the army theme that attracts Amis too, the stark collision of male personalities and desires, unmitigated by any female distraction or softening. Nor should one overlook the persistence in Amis's discourse of handy army locutions. Leslie Fiedler, he notes, lays out his critical kit for inspection, and in an essay about conventional literary characters, the reader hears of "a course of P. T.," "the wakey-wakey man," and "demobilization." At the end of the essay, Amis ushers off the topic with the command, "DIS-*MISS!*"

Amis has considered more carefully than most the moral consequences of institutional life, in the university as well as the army. Of the army he has observed that "in an organization where there must be unquestioning obedience there must be passive injustice," and he goes on to consider some of the unfortunate consequences of the military life. "The qualities necessary for being a successful soldier are comparatively few. They are only a selection of the qualities necessary for making a successful anything else, including a human being." But if the "Yes, sir" environment is certain, over the long term, to shrivel originality and constrict thought, Amis admits that military situations still offer unique moral trials. While acknowledging that "military glory is all nonsense," still "it is glorious not to run away." In addition, it is undeniable that fortitude, as in Aristotle's day, is still a virtue, and so is "not letting one's side down." Hence Amis's scorn for the unpatriotic behavior of the Audens and Isherwoods, not to mention the Blunts and the Philbys, of this world.

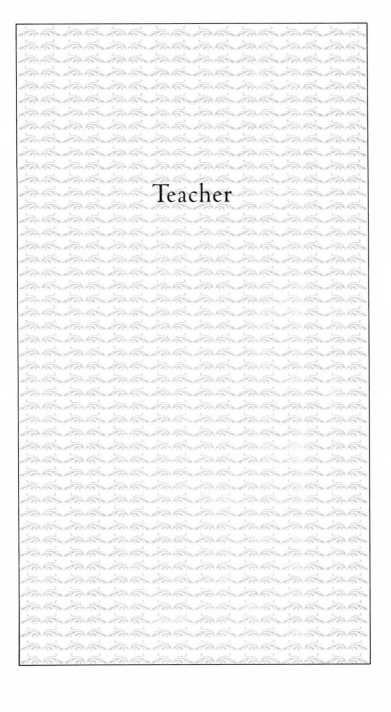

Teacher

EDUCATED by family, school, university, and army, Amis was prepared for—what? Teaching, of course, and the writing of novels, of course. But also for the work appropriate to his simultaneous career as man of letters.

John Gross's definition is succinct and telling. A man of letters is "a serious critic operating outside the academic fold." He, or she, is that apparent paradox, an "intellectual journalist." Gross is interested in critics and literary commentators positioned halfway between the scientism and pedantry of the university approach to literature and the mass media's understanding of art and its uses. Between, that is, boredom, on the one hand, and "entertainment," on the other. Gross himself, editor, critic, private scholar, author of the elegant and valuable *The Rise and Fall of the Man of Letters* (1969, reissued with new material, 1991), is a fine contemporary example. One of the earliest was probably Samuel Johnson, soon followed by William Hazlitt, who can easily be regarded by his successors as the patron saint and all-time hero of the profession. Gross reminds the contemporary reader of the way, once upon a time, distinguished literary criticism, some by Coleridge verging on metaphysics, appeared in popular or almost popular, periodicals. In the nineteenth century such periodicals were a normal part of the literary scene. Magazines like the *Edinburgh Review*, the *Quarterly*, *Blackwood's*, the *London Review*, the *Westminster Review*, the *Cornhill Magazine* (where the essays constituting Arnold's *Culture and Anarchy* first appeared), the *Fortnightly Review*, *The Nineteenth Century*, the

Saturday Review, and the *Adelphi.* Later, there was *The Bookman, The New Age,* the *Nation,* the *Athenaeum,* and later still, in the twentieth century, the London *Times Literary Supplement,* the *New Statesman,* and the *Spectator.*

It was these periodicals that published the popular literary commentary and talk about books by Walter Bagehot, Leslie Stephen, John Morley, Andrew Lang, and George Saintsbury—who resembles Amis in his dual devotion to wine and literature. (Amis notes of Saintsbury that he was "debarred by nature from writing anything not worth reading.") Another contributor to the bookish sort of periodical was the man of letters Havelock Ellis, in his day known not just as a "sexologist" but as the scholarly editor of the esteemed Mermaid Series, presenting the texts of early English dramatists. There were such non-university critics as Edmund Gosse, Austin Dobson, and J. Middleton Murry, and novelists like Arnold Bennett did not disdain tasks of editing, reviewing, and general literary commentary. Edmund Blunden was an exemplary bookman in the same tradition. Best known as a "creative writer," namely, a poet, he was at the same time a critic, a biographer, a literary scholar, and a collector, rescuer, and editor-preserver of unjustly forgotten writers. In the variety of his interests and the copiousness of his production, Robert Graves could also stand as a model modern man of letters, issuing essays, memoirs, translations, "scholarship," and criticism, together with poems and novels. Other British examples are Julian Symons, critic, biographer of Carlyle and Poe, historian of crime writing, and William Plomer. Plomer, although known as the author of five novels and six volumes of short stories, published also fourteen volumes of poetry, three of autobiography, one opera libretto, and introductions to works by Gissing, Conrad, Melville, and Rose Macaulay, and in his spare time he edited the diary of the Victorian cleric Francis Kilvert and published it in three volumes. As Amis says, "Any proper writer ought to be able to write anything, from an Easter Day sermon to a sheepdip handout."

Before, and even well after the study of English literature

became a university subject, many of these literary people had nothing to do with universities. Their training was rather in "high journalism." Gosse didn't attend a university, and neither did such later writers as Wyndham Lewis and George Orwell. The British tradition that a man of letters, if clever, needn't waste time on a conventional literary education was honored by the late Terence Kilmartin, literary editor of the *Observer* and distinguished translator of Proust, and by Michael Holroyd, biographer of Lytton Strachey and Bernard Shaw. Addressing the topic of his curious lack of university education, Holroyd has said, "My subjects have been my professors." And there were once American men of letters who pursued their vocation quite outside universities. H. L. Mencken, of course, and Edmund Wilson and Malcolm Cowley. And one doesn't want to neglect the numerous distinguished British women of letters, whose professional venue is London periodicals rather than educational institutions, women like Hilary Spurling, biographer of I. Compton-Burnett; Victoria Glendinning, biographer of Trollope, Edith Sitwell, and Vita Sackville-West; as well as Naomi Lewis, Claire Tomalin, and Janet Adam Smith, onetime editor of the BBC's *The Listener* and literary editor of the *New Statesman.*

The archetype of the contemporary woman of letters is Virginia Woolf, whose university was neither Oxford, Cambridge, nor London but the books she reviewed for the *Times Literary Supplement.* Comparable in few other respects, Amis and Virginia Woolf are similar in this: each is a "novelist," but each is a great deal more, and it's possible that the greater distinction and honor resides in the more. If Woolf's total production is considered, and more important, experienced, her novels seem to reduce to their proper weight and her eminence as a woman of letters begins to become clear, her undeniable excellence as an author of essays, letters, diaries, reviews, biography, and inquiries into literary history. To emphasize unduly the simplified current meaning of *creative* and to insist that she be regarded primarily as a novelist may implicitly demean her, locating her with, say, Dorothy Richardson, not to mention such "women novelists" of her time as Pearl Buck and Margaret Mitchell. Unlike these people, Woolf is an imaginative epistemologist and a profound thinker about perception, memory, philosophy, history, and art and aesthetics in general. She is a mind turned novelist, just as Amis is a critic and literary sensorium turned story-teller. And in Amis, as in George Orwell, the essay sometimes intervenes and rather upsets the novel. The threat of the novel to the career of letters can be seen in the mess Orwell's *A Clergyman's Daughter* became, where essays frequently burst into the fictional milieu, violating narrative credibility and stalling fictional progress and pace.

A similar effect is visible in Amis's novel *The Russian Girl.* In the first fifteen pages alone, the narrative seems to yield momentarily while Amis indulges four of his essayistic topics: the collapse of serious university study; women and their affectations; language as an indicator of self-designated eccentricity; and the awfulness of pretentious restaurants. Lurking within the narrative prose is another essay topic: the predominance of industrial noises in the modern world, the rumble of heavy vehicles, the impertinent racket of passing aircraft, especially helicopters, the whole making the modern urban scene a virtual hell on earth. It's as if the contemporary world has been designed as a conspiracy against the sensitive.

This essayistic impulse, entirely appropriate for the man of letters, is what causes some of Amis's novels to resemble not so much fictions as anthologies of opinions, with the fiction serving as mere carriage or cement. Indeed, Amis may seem the most "opinionated" novelist now writing. But there is a complication and comfort. If Amis's fiction is compromised by opinions, so is Flaubert's.

Although Karl Miller has taught in universities, his identity is essentially that of a man of letters, and he is most widely known as an essayist and as the editor of *The London Review of Books.* Looking back on the unique flowering in Britain, in the nineteenth century, of the tradition of the high-journalistic man of letters, he agrees with John Gross about its main cause. It's in large part a result of a remarkably homogeneous general education which assumed that everyone had been granted possession of the same truisms about ancient history and heroism and nobility; about British and Continental history; and about all the copybook maxims—and their easily satirized reversals. Homogeneity of minds is one reason London still has a high-journalistic literary culture, while—no surprise—heterogeneity is the reason New York lacks one. Another reason is the BBC, which provides a haven and income for people of letters without forcing upon them the specialization universities demand. On the radio, one must be accessible to the audience, aware constantly of addressing the (intelligent) common listener. Thanks to the cultural ambitions of the BBC, the designation *broadcaster* is still significant in Britain, although virtually obsolete in America.

Without engaging in snobbish contrasts or falling for sentimental reactionary Anglophilia of the English-Speaking-Union kind, it's hard not to notice the assumptions writers can entertain about British readers which make quality literary journalism possible there. For example, it would be hard to imagine this headline, from a story about a vain pop star, appearing in the *New York Times:*

Et in Arcadia Very Big Ego

Independent, June 7, 1992

A headline on an article about the female sexual organs assumes a literate reader familiar with at least some tag-lines of modern poetry:

Today We Have Naming of Parts

Observer, June 31, 1992

Again, a headline on an article about a forestry scheme:

Fresh Woods and Tax Breaks New?

Observer, March 8, 1992

Shakespeare is assumed to be possessed by more people than those who teach in or attend schools and universities. Hence the sculptor John White titling a work depicting a young hoodlum, "But Soft, What Lout through Yonder Window Breaks?" (*Independent,* March

49

11, 1992). Another headline depends for its force on the reader's knowing, and liking, Stevie Smith's poem "Not Waving but Drowning" (*Independent,* March 14, 1992). I may be mistaken, but I don't think any American newspaper, or virtually any other publication, for that matter, could get away with such a headline as

A Poet! He Hath Put His Heart to School

above a story in the *Guardian* (May 5, 1992) about a school poetry and arts festival. And there's a popular interest in verbalism and having fun with it not found in the USA. Witty left-wingers like to locate billboards advertising cars or holidays, things appealing largely to the monied classes, and to alter the message by pasting sheets printed in the same type and style over the original. Very funny, very credible, and quite undetectable except to the sophisticated who recognize and enjoy the altered sense. Thus, to a billboard ad for an automobile headed SAVE MONEY, the leftish wits add the words DON'T PAY YOUR POLL TAX. That suggests the atmosphere of high literacy, which if perhaps something of a fiction, is sufficiently ubiquitous and accepted to sustain a special journalistic literary culture where non-university talents can still flourish.

During the nineteenth century, there were probably few English men and women involved with writing who did not assume that English literature is the greatest in the world and that British superiority in letters amply compensates for deficiencies in such other arts as music and painting. They would also assume that contact with English literature, given the continual weakening of the church, yielded inestimable spiritual, moral, and asethetic benefits. Shakespeare was of course one reason for local pride: English is the only modern European literature with so brilliant and unclassifiable an original in it. The sense that English literature is unique helped sustain a strong tradition of enthusiastic amateurism in scholarship, with plenty of room for non-academic scholars and critics. Because of its insularity and the native conviction that English literature is too great to be sullied by close analysis, Britain was much later than Continental countries in professionalizing approaches to literature by founding academies and learned journals: the *Review of English Studies* began only in 1925. It's no surprise that the idea persists in England that the man of letters and the university scholar are antithetical types, and the notion dies hard that literary understanding is quite possible among what Walter Bagehot called "the illogical classes," ordinary people unassisted by learned guidance.

No one comparing British with Continental scholarship and literary commentary can help noticing how often it has been divorced from academies and universities. Such landmarks of multi-volume late-Victorian scholarship as the *Dictionary of National Biography* and the *Dictionary of Music* were conducted by people distant from universities, Leslie Stephen, on the one hand, and George Grove, on the other. John Gross observes of Grove that he "began his career in building a lighthouse in Jamaica at the age of twenty-two and crowned it by editing his famous *Dictionary of Music* (a subject in which he was entirely self-taught)." The two most impressive proprietors of English literature in the early twentieth century, George Saintsbury and Arthur Quiller-Couch, arrived at their positions not through academic training but through journalism. After taking a second-class Oxford degree, Saintsbury worked as an essayist and reviewer for periodicals for most of his life. He was fifty years old when, in 1895, he was appointed Regius Professor at the University of Edinburgh. And when Quiller-Couch was designated Professor of English at Cambridge in 1912, his preparation had been not that of a scholar but a journalist, a popular novelist, and a writer of adventure stories. Like Saintsbury, he was intensely patriotic, and his patriotism, Gross says, took the form of "a thorough dislike of the German quasi-scientific approach to English." It is thus hardly surprising that until very recently the British resisted the Continental and American tradition that the advanced study of literature leads to a doctoral degree, and actually the formal academic study of native vernacular literature began very late in England. The literary scholar Basil Willey has recalled that when he returned to Cambridge after the Great

War, he found the veterans insisting that the curriculum be adapted to their demands—more English to read, less Greek and Latin. "The founding of the Cambridge English School," Willey says, "was symbolical of this. It is perhaps not generally known that the first Tripos [the first Honors examination] in English as a university subject, was held in 1919."

With that as a background, one appreciates the special British instinct for keeping literature from being pawed over or scientized at universities and made into something to be examined on rather than enjoyed. John Gross has posed a question seldom ventured in the United States but not unheard in the United Kingdom:

> Isn't there a certain basic antagonism between the very nature of a university and the very spirit of literature? The academic mind is cautious, tightly organized, fault-finding, competitive—and above all aware of other academic minds. . . . Think of the whole idea of regarding literature as a *discipline.* Literature can be strenuous or difficult or deeply disturbing; it can be a hundred things—but a discipline is not one of them. Discipline means compulsion, and an interest in literature thrives on spontaneity, eager curiosity, the anticipation of pleasure; it is unlikely that a reader who comes to a book under duress, or weighed down with a sense of duty, will ever really *read* it at all, however much he may learn about it. Even the most intensely serious literature needs to be approached with a certain lightness of heart, if it is to yield its full intensity.

From this position it's only a step to journalist Paul Johnson's conviction that "universities are the most overrated institutions of our age." Focusing on what goes on in English departments, Johnson implies that the only thing they ever offered that was necessary—that is, that a non-university reader couldn't master on his own—was Anglo-Saxon, but now Anglo-Saxon is being dropped in favor of various sorts of "literary theory." Anglo-Saxon was made compulsory in the first place "because old-fashioned academics thought taking a degree in English was a soft option anyway—which it is—and should be stiffened by forcing the un-dergraduates to do something hard. Take away Anglo-Saxon and there is nothing left but idleness and an increasing clutter of nonsense . . . all expressed in hideous jargon." Views like Gross's and Johnson's come very close to Amis's, but he arrived at his empirically after fourteen years of "teaching English" at universities. He declares that it was the sight and sound of academic staff relaxing in the Senior Common Room at University College, Leicester, where Larkin was once librarian, that provided the seed for the satire in *Lucky Jim.* In his early innocence, Amis found it almost unbelievable that there could be such people—all that complacency, eccentricity, and egotism. It's sometimes overlooked that *Lucky Jim* is specifically a satire on the sort of thought and behavior not just found at but apparently encouraged at a university: laziness, vanity, cultural and intellectual affectation, self-absorption, and sycophancy. As literary scholar and novelist Gilbert Phelps has pointed out, "one of the purposes in putting Jim Dixon in a new redbrick university is to show that what might have been a fresh start was already infiltrated by the old Oxbridge values and assumptions so notably embodied in Professor Welch."

Amis has taught at four universities, and his experience at each seems to have augmented his disillusion with that scene. He quite liked teaching at University College, Swansea, from 1949 to 1961. The students were unpretentious and friendly and some seemed actually to have an interest in literature. Although the work was harder than expected—discovering how much time it took to prepare a half-decent lecture was a surprise—he liked the college and he liked Swansea: "I miss it constantly and I miss those days." Teaching poetry to eager or at least neutral young people was one of his pleasures, but another, easily overlooked, was the pleasure of simply being young, starting a family, and realizing that life lay ahead, not behind. He found the faculty of the small English department in the main amiable and conscientious, and some were even interested in literature. One thing the college offered was a chance to witness Dylan Thomas in action as a speaker and celebrated personality when Thomas gave a talk and reading sponsored by the English Society of the college. As a poet, Thomas's defects seem to Amis to be grave, attributable largely to egotism and affectation. "Apart from just one poem, 'The Hunchback in the Park,' which distinguishes itself from all the rest of his poetic output by not being about him, and a few isolated lines from other poems . . . he strikes me as a very bad poet indeed, or else a brilliant one in a mode that is anathema to me. Either way he is a pernicious figure, one who has helped to get Wales and Welsh poetry a bad name and generally done lasting harm to both." As a performer, Amis found Thomas's voice magnificent "and his belief in what he read," whether his own or others' poems, "seemed absolute," yet Thomas's performance was needlessly affected and melodramatic, "naked showing-off."

In 1958 Amis had his second taste of university teaching, this time at Princeton, where for a year he taught "creative writing" during his first delightful visit to America. It took only the spectacle of Manhattan and "the wondrous multi-colored lights of the New Jersey Turnpike," together with the soon-to-be-enjoyed amiability and generosity with drink of the local academics, to persuade him that "this was my second country and always would be." At Princeton his student writing group consisted of a couple of dozen: one aspirant playwright, one ditto poet, and the rest prose fiction practitioners. He worked with them individually. The poet once told him, when Amis suggested that something in one of his submissions wouldn't be clear to the reader, "Sir, I don't pay much heed to the reader." After that, Amis reports, "I ceased to pay more heed to him than I had to." He was impressed by the amount of talent on show and thought the best student writing exciting and "promising," but he now sees that he mistook for genuine literary talent "high intelligence and a sense of purpose." Only one of his students flowered into a writer, the playwright, who actually had one of his works performed.

In addition to this writing class, he also had to teach a weekly class (dignified, in the local jargon, as a "preceptorial") devoted to general critical principles. The text was a collection of short stories. His experience with James's *The Aspern Papers* persuaded him that "most American literature is a disaster," and that to teach it at the expense of better British stuff is to play up to the chauvinistic anxiety and philistinism at the heart of the general American department of English. And while dealing with American authors Amis understood something important that distinguished them from British, their penchant for self-destruction: "Writers and artists in [America] seem destined to be or become stricken deer, misfits, assorted victims and freaks, drunks rather than mere drinkers, hermits, suicides."

Because his stipend at Princeton proved not to go very far, he eked it out by doing considerable lecturing in the vicinity. The lecture was always the same, "Problems of a Comic Novelist," and it contained the memorable declaration, "The funniest thing in the world is solemnity." Sometimes he gave the lecture far afield, at the University of Illinois, for example, which soon persuaded him that nothing of interest takes place there, ever took place, or ever could take place. This conviction led him to a conclusion about mass education: "When a country is so rich that it can afford to send a great many or most of its youngsters to universities if it feels like it, some of those universities will be places like Princeton or Harvard, but a hell of a lot more of them will be like the one at Champaign-Urbana." That is, because there isn't enough real intellect or curiosity to go around, obviously its presence must very often be faked.

Suspecting that more lecturing might be required of him at Princeton, he had taken the precaution of bringing along his notes for his Swansea course on the history of criticism. But the famous Christian Gauss Seminar in Literary Criticism, to which he was supposed to contribute, that year was focusing on popular culture, with participants like Dwight Macdonald. At a lunch with R. P. Blackmur, the director of the Gauss Seminars, it was suggested that Amis talk about science fiction, having a reputation as an enthusiast for that genre. The result was six lectures and ultimately the book *New Maps of Hell* (1960), which, Amis maintains, helped raise science fiction "to the status of a branch of culture." That, alas, led to its authors growing increasingly pretentious "and so to its eventual undoing."

Princeton offered him a two-year extension of his appointment, and he was tempted to say yes. But he realized that to stay longer would entail a wholly American education for his children, and "I muttered to myself about being thirty-seven, just too old to set about becoming an American, which was what was really at stake." Returning to England, he took with him images of America's abundance and variety, the immense "energy, generosity, and good will" he had been shown, as well as mementoes of American ugliness, squalor, and violence. (If there was Princeton, there was also Trenton.) Remembering scenes of startling natural beauty he grows lyrical: "For instance, upstate New York, like North Wales but grander, greenness, spaciousness, tallness, bright sun on snow," and he adds, "How I should like to see it all again as it was then."

He closed down his teaching career at Swansea in 1961, when the University of Cambridge offered him the job of Director of English Studies at Peterhouse. He now realizes that what caused him to accept this offer was a romantic hope that Cambridge would be like Oxford when he was young. "I should have known better, not being a young man any more." What he found—was he more critical now?—was snobbery, provincialism, and shop- rather than literary talk. It was perhaps the chic academic dinner parties at Cambridge that finally wore him down, together with atmospheres and attitudes he recalls without pleasure more than thirty years later. He was dining once at the high table of another college, when the talk became stalled on the topic of the costly engravings, drawings, and so on the diners had recently bought. "Noticing, presumably, that I had nothing whatever to contribute to this discussion, another guest asked me, 'And what is *your* particular, er, line of country in this, er?' With Grand Guignol humility of tone and gesture, I said, 'I'm afraid I don't sort of go in for any of that kind of thing.' The other man said . . . , 'I think that's a dreadful thing to say.'"

That suggests one reason Amis and Cambridge couldn't get on.

Another was the general adulation of the Cambridge critic F. R. Leavis, whose vigorously self-righteous, moralistic, badly written work, in effect totalitarian, "seems to me," Amis says, "to have done more harm than good to literature, never mind the study of literature." Leavis was reported to have said of Amis's arrival that Peterhouse could no longer be taken seriously, having "given a fellowship to a *pornographer.*"

(What could he have had in mind? The chastity and cleanliness of Amis's writings has always been conspicuous and has doubtless done them damage with readers in the 1970s and '80s, expecting the erotic details available in other fiction of the period. An example of Amis's care in this matter is the scene of the seduction of the boy Peter Furneaux by Mrs. Trevelyan in *The Riverside Villas Murder* (1973). A few kisses and hugs are specified, but there are no details about copulation, although it's clear that during the afternoon in question three separate acts have occurred. Exciting enough, for those who can read with active imaginations.)

Now that he was writing fiction (he was at work on *One Fat Englishman*) and making more money from it, and having more fun, than from his association with Peterhouse, he began to feel academically overworked, although he enjoyed the tutorials with one or two at a time of his eight or ten students. These or similar literary conversations took place sometimes in pubs, and his appearance there with one or another of his younger charges occasioned the whisper that he was a homosexual—so little was it credible at Cambridge that talk about literature might be what he was engaged in. These tutorials on literary questions seem the only thing Amis misses, now, about teaching. These tutorials, he says, "offered the only context I have found in which serious, detailed and exhaustive discussion of literature is socially practicable. You cannot say in your club or dining-room, 'Let's have a look at what Eve actually tells Adam about her conversation with the serpent' without at best seeing the other fellow's eyes glaze over." But Amis knew now that he was rather a writer than a teacher. He resigned his fellowship and moved to London, where he has lived ever since.

Of Cambridge he says, "I should never have gone there." He had at first imputed to Cambridge a certain intellectual power, but in this respect he found it "markedly inferior to Swansea."

But there was to be one final immersion in the life of the professor of English, in 1967. For some time, ever since his acquaintance with Princeton, he had been friendly with an amiable young Princeton professor, Russell Fraser, a Renaissance scholar and Shakespearian. Fraser, who had moved on to become chairman of the English department at Vanderbilt University, in Nashville, Tennessee, invited Amis to come to Vanderbilt for one semester to teach modern British literature. At first Amis, who could think only of lynchings and stupid country music, naturally concluded that a grateful refusal was in order. But considering the lightness of the teaching load offered and recalling the fun he'd once had with Fraser and his wife—interesting people, and attractive social drinkers—he finally accepted and crossed on the *Queen Mary*.

Not surprisingly, Nashville appalled him, with its bogus Parthenon, its ugly outcrops of bad religious sculpture and architecture, its curious blue laws regulating the consumption of drink, and its terrible restaurants, two only, "one providing bad, the other very bad food and service." The heat and unaccustomed sweatiness were an unpleasant surprise too. The public segregation of the races, about which he had heard a lot, proved all too true, despite official arrangements and pretenses to the contrary. He assumed that attitudes inside the university, among the educated, traveled, and civilized, would be different. A couple of academic parties illuminated him.

One was given by Professor of English Walter Sullivan, and in many respects it was a lovely party, with good and ample food and drink, together with lots of cordiality and conversation. But the conversation tended to stick with the favorite subject, the "problem" of the blacks assignable to, among other things, their "mental, moral, and social" deficiencies, and the necessity of keeping them down. One of the most ardent speakers on this subject was Professor Sullivan himself, who summed up the conversation this way, and Amis swears this is exactly what he said: "I can't find it in my heart to give a negro [pron. *nigra*] or a Jew an A." At which point Amis breaks in to remind the reader that those unbelievable words were spoken by a university teacher, and, I will add, the holder of an honorary degree from the Episcopal Theological Seminary in Kentucky. Amis at first assumed that Sullivan was being ironic or was mimicking some awful other person and almost said something like, "You do it marvellously, Walter—for a moment there I thought you really. . . ." But no one in the group said anything like that, only "It was real good to hear that said, time people faced facts, they wouldn't stand for being pushed any further, *thank you* for saying that, Walter." Amis adds that Walter Sullivan was one among several of his neighbors who celebrated the murder of John F. Kennedy by throwing a party. On another Vanderbilt social occasion, the wife of the Professor of Iberian Languages wondered how a "real lady" like Desdemona could have forgot herself so far as to marry a "black mayun" like Othello.

It may be said here that one illusion of the well-intentioned young that is slow to erode and finally disappear is the conviction, which they tend to embrace during their schooling at all levels, that the well-educated, indeed, the learned, are somehow if not better, at least wiser than other people, more immune to cruelty, intolerance, prejudice, and egotism. If not, what's the use of liberal studies? If not, why spend time with Plato and Cicero, Socrates and Jesus, Aquinas and Pascal? Are virtue and wisdom to be grasped only theoretically, like mathematical principles? Do they not feed action? Like most young people of intellectual bent, Amis found the disturbing answers by repeated experience among the learned and those close to them. As a moralist requiring honesty of others as of himself, it's hardly his fault that they so often failed to rise to their proclaimed standards of moral and intellectual distinction.

Despite such bizarre moments as these, Amis's stay at Vanderbilt was in part redeemed by the students, to whom he lectured on the Modern British Novel. "The class was about the best I have ever taught: punctual, polite, attentive, ready but not overready with questions and objections, containing the ingredient essential for a decent course . . . , however much the lecturer may squirm at its presence: a couple of students of whom he is very slightly afraid." At the end of the course Amis asked the class which of the novels they'd read they had enjoyed the most. Waugh's *Decline and Fall* won, just as it had at Swansea. The validation of works by the enjoyment of the common reader was still for Amis something that mattered a lot. But all in all, the whole four months came close to a nightmare, a period "second only to my army service," Amis says, "as the one in my life I would least soon relive."

His fourteen years of acquaintance with universities left him with a number of convictions classifiable under such heads as *futility* and *fraud* and *pretentiousness*. Amis never managed to reconcile himself to the consequence of the vast expansion of the universities that took place in the 1960s and 1970s: hordes of students quite unprepared by intellectual interests or even simple curiosity for the university experience. And of course sadly ignorant—to Amis's shock, many proved never to have heard of *meter* in poetry. But still, they had been encouraged to write in the way wonderfully caught by Simon Gray in his play *Butley*. An essay on *The Winter's Tale* read aloud by Butley's student Miss Heasman sounds like this:

> "Hermione's re-awakening—the statue restored to life after a winter of sixteen years' duration—is in reality Leontes's re-awakening, spiritually, and of course the most moving exemplification of both the revitalization theme and thus of forgiveness on the theological as well as the human level."

"Level?" asks Butley. "The human *'level'?*" But she proceeds:

> "The central image is drawn from nature, to counterpoint the imagery of the first half of the play, with its stress on sickness and deformity. Paradoxically, *A Winter's Tale* of a frozen soul . . . is therefore thematically and symbolically about revitalization. . . . In this context it might be said that Leontes represents the affliction that is universal, and so contingently human evil, and in this sense, the sense of a shared blight—"

Silently appalled, Butley asks her to jump to the end, "so we can get the feel of your conclusion." She does so:

> "So just as the seasonal winter was the winter of the soul, so is the seasonal spring the spring of the soul. The imagery changes from disease to floral, the tone from mad bitterness to joyfulness. As we reach the play's climax we feel our own—spiritual—sap rising."

Gray is a master of what he's aping there, having taught English for some time at Queen Mary College, University of London. Any teacher of English, and certainly Amis, is deeply acquainted with such bullshit, and with the teacher's awareness that he can't do anything about it, the fault lying too deep for correction. The teacher's choice is either a whole career of silent, bored acquiescence, or quitting. Few quit.

For Amis, student and faculty insistence on "relevance" is another symptom that the spirit of learning is rare in the university. As he explains, "The student who . . . is looking for relevance is looking for vocational training, a harmless desire in itself, though anti-academic and therefore not to be indulged at a university; the teacher who wants to import it is an enemy of culture." But if most university students are not really students in Amis's terms, they do become skilled in practices which will become indispensable in later life. Amis recalls the way students of English at Oxford behaved in his day. Very few had any ear for literature, or talent for understanding it, or impulse to treasure it. They treated it "as a pure commodity, a matter for evasion and fraud, confidence trickery to filch a degree." What was important was not reading and delighting in literature but winning "the coming battle of wits with the examiners." Amis sees it now as all a cynical game, far removed from any real mastery of literary aesthetics historically considered, with more attention lavished on Foucault, Derrida, and Lacan than on Ben Jonson, George Eliot, or Tennyson. ("The 'research' which counts most in literature is simply reading a great deal."—John Gross) Most teachers of literature, Amis has gathered, are people of "foggy aesthetic sense, the ideal audience for their own propaganda." That's why for years they insisted on the literary rather than merely antiquarian interest of Old English poetry, and that's why now they can hear and utter without embarrassment barbarous mock-scientific baboo language like *intertextuality, orality, narratology,* and *marginality.* The sort of university talk Amis rightly despises is committed by Professor John B. Vickery, of the University of California at Riverside, commenting on Amis's short story "Who or What Was It?" This story, says Professor Vickery, "holds the chief clue to Amis's discovery of and fascination with intertextuality as its own species of the hermeneutic circle." No one would think of asking a man of letters, "What critical approach are you using?" or "Which literary theory is your critical operation based on?" But daily you can hear such questions asked around university English departments. And in an atmosphere, in addition, of covert envy and overt contempt. Amis says, "I don't remember ever hearing a charitable word spoken about anyone at Oxford."

As a result of his teaching experience, Amis is alert also to the bad habits professors get into from addressing students captive in classrooms, where attention need not, as with men of letters, be earned by charm, wit, or eloquence, but can be compelled by the implicit threat of low grades. In Amis and Robert Conquest's *The Egyptologists* there is a knowledgeable send-up of professorial discourse, the sort of speech appropriate to a lifetime spent explaining things to the slow-witted or uninterested. "Don's delivery" it is designated, featuring the enunciation of platitudes at the slowest possible speed. Reminiscent of Amis's time at Cambridge? After all this, it seems not hard to understand Amis's point, often reiterated, that in English-speaking universities English literature should not be taught at all.

Critic

I N *Double Agent: The Critic and Society* (1992), a book
mainly about American critics of the Amis "social" type
but dealing also with such British non-academics as Orwell, Cyril Connolly, and John Gross, Morris Dickstein
specifies three characteristics of genuine criticism, as opposed to "literary theory":

1. Criticism is *writing,* and writing in language that is itself
worth attending to, that itself becomes part of the pleasure of
explanation or valuation. "Its first goal is to interest and hold its
readers." That is, it is an aesthetic act, like literature, but unlike
"scholarship" or the conveyance of information.

2. Criticism is "personal or it is nothing." Which seems to
imply the third characteristic,

3. "Like art, it is a social activity." It "seeks subtly to change
the world, starting with the mind of the reader."

Those last words suggest that Amis's criticism might be in Dickstein's mind, but Amis, presumably because he's "a novelist,"
makes no appearance in his book.

Beginning in 1955, Amis was writing criticism for a wide range
of London periodicals, including *Encounter,* the *New Statesman,* the
Twentieth Century, the *Observer,* and pre-eminently, the *Spectator.* It
soon became clear to readers that Amis's essays and reviews were
something new, if the newness was not yet, perhaps, clearly defin-
able. But journalist Harry Ritchie saw what was unique: "Those
reviews for the *Spectator* in the fifties were exceptional for a colloquial tone and a critical rigor far removed from the belletristic

approach that still dominated the literary sections of the press."
(What critic before Amis dared refer to writers and their readers as
chaps, or works of literature as *stuff?* What critic before Amis
addressed the reader as *mate?*) Soon other critics and commentators
were imitating the no-nonsense, can-the-bullshit tone, with the
result that, as Ritchie says, Amis's criticism "had a profound effect
on postwar English writing." Amis was re-introducing the archaic
critical virtues of skepticism and honesty as a counterweight to
publicity, cant, critical affectation, and cultural orthodoxies. He
was also bringing to non-academic criticism a refreshing focus on
literature itself as the subject of interest—rather than on literature
as an auxiliary to politics, ideology, or manners.

While others were requiring of literature some sort of "commitment"—one of the sacred words of the 1950s—Amis was saying, "No 'commitment' for me, except to literature." And now,
forty years later, the literary dimension of literature still takes
precedence. Amis liked his neighbor Peter Quennell, but got a bit
annoyed by Quennell's apparent disinclination to talk about literature instead of something adjacent. In their conversations, Amis
reports, "Time and time again I [would] try to keep the focus on,
say, *The Village,* and Peter [would] shift it languidly but inexorably
to Crabbe's opium addiction." The more one attends to Amis's
criticism, the more one agrees with his view that almost no one in
the contemporary world, in or out of universities, is really interested in literature, something else always being substituted as a
subject more worthy of interest, whether historical data or myth,
biography, politics, an author's attitude towards revolution or sex,
and the like. In addition, Amis was perhaps the first intelligent
British critic to bring his wide command of literature, as well as his
wit, to the task of seriously opposing the critical orthodoxy of
Modernism. Stuffy critics had been doing this for some time, but
Amis was something different, young, clever, militant, funny, non-
academic, and supremely forthright and courageous.

What was this literary Modernism that Amis set out to under-
mine? It was the late nineteenth- and early twentieth-century theo-

retical war against the received, the bourgeois, the sentimental, the didactic, and the democratic. Those conscious of engaging in the exciting new movement of artistic Modernism were happy to oppose the "realism" of Victorian and Georgian writing and painting. These artifacts were too close to life itself, and since life was not art, art had to be markedly different. It had to advertise its difference by stylization, conspicuous artifice, abstraction, leanings towards the geometrical, and moral uselessness. The Modernist thinker T. E. Hulme stigmatized as the enemy the "vital," that is, the lifelike, literature and art of the nineteenth century, urging its replacement by the geometrical. (The novelty of what was being proposed can be estimated by imagining Blunden's "Lonely Love" rendered in a de-humanized version.)

In addition, there is audible in Modernist literary behavior an undertone of crude anger which is entirely un-Amisian. This is the characteristic note of Modernist artistic manifestoes like Wyndham Lewis's *BLAST:* "BLAST humor—Quack English drug for stupidity and sleepiness." Shrill adversary tonalities echo even in the private letters of committed Modernists, odd because private letters are normally a literary form associated with charm and even courtesy. D. H. Lawrence afire with self-righteousness is a good example of Modernist fury in action. Imagine Amis saying of the residents of Taormina that they are *"Canaille, canaglia, Schweinhunderei,* stink-pots. Pfui!—pish, pshaw, prrr! They all stink in my nostrils." Ezra Pound is another to whom murderous images come easily. "I personally would not feel myself guilty of manslaughter," he says, "if by any miracle I ever had the pleasure of killing [Henry Seidel] Canby [editor of the stick-in-the-mud *Saturday Review of Literature*] or the editor of the *Atlantic Monthly* and their replicas, and of ordering a wholesale death and/or deportation of a great number of affable, suave, moderate men."

As that suggests, there is built into Modernism a hatred—and that is not too strong a word—of ordinary people, and one traditional genre of painting with which Modernism will have no truck is sympathetic portraiture, which is incompatible with the new emphasis on style rather than representation as the essence of art. José Ortega y Gasset, one of Modernism's most intelligent and powerful spokesmen, puts it this way: "Preoccupation with the human content of the work is in principle incompatible with aesthetic enjoyment proper." It used to be different, he admits: "With the things represented on traditional paintings we could have imaginary [sexual] intercourse. Many a young Englishman has fallen in love with [the Mona Lisa]. With the objects of modern pictures no intercourse is possible." Or, to turn from painting to poetry, with which of Eliot's characters could you fall in love, or even admire? Hardly Madame Sosostris, the late-drinking pub wives or the hysterical high-society woman, the damaged, passive Thames maidens, the unfeeling typist, the perverse Mr. Eugenides, or the brutal Sweeney. In the same way, what response except satiric contempt seems called for by Pound's Mr. Nixon or Lady Valentine? It was this general disdain for people, and people of all sorts, that the Assistant Lecturer in English at Swansea increasingly found offensive in Modernist writings, highly touted though they might be and increasingly a solid part of the university English curriculum. One reason Amis likes Auden, Modernist though he can be at times, is that, unlike Eliot, he can write love poems.

Lawrence in particular Amis singles out, in a review of his criticism, as one of the great Modernist haters of "the mass," regarding himself as one of the elect. "And what are we to do, all the rest of us, the mass? Can we become superior too? Hardly, because it's all a matter of feeling, you see. Thinking . . . won't help. It only makes matters worse. Some are born to sweet delight. Very few." What makes much of Lawrence's criticism valueless except to connoisseurs of eccentric and egotistical moments is the constant intrusion of his "private obsession" and his Modernist will to power over others. Those searching for useful sense in Lawrence will find not much more than "egomania, fatuity, and gimcrack theorizing," and plenty of Modernist "bitterness and censoriousness too."

These strictures can be found in *What Became of Jane Austen and*

Other Questions, the collection of fifteen years of his critical pieces Amis published in 1970. These essays, dealing with authors from Austen to Philip Roth and Vladimir Nabokov, exhibit precisely the characteristics attributed to Lawrence by his admirers, "utter and transparent honesty, . . . indifference to academic and journalistic procedures, and above all, what Dr. Leavis describes as [Lawrence's] 'power of distinguishing his own feeling and emotions from conventional sentiment.'" That most of the literary essays in this collection began as reviews is not to their discredit: so did, say, Eliot's "The Metaphysical Poets," which powerfully influenced the taste of a generation.

It is in the first essay in the book that the reader finds Amis registering "the power of distinguishing his own feelings and emotions from conventional sentiment." Conventional sentiment, especially among cultish, sentimental Janeites inside and outside of universities, is likely to hold that Jane Austen is as admirable morally as she is artistically. Amis thinks differently, at least about her attitude toward the behavior of her characters in *Mansfield Park.* Amis finds Austen indeed a moralist, but a moralist with socially offensive habits, "a habit of censoriousness where there ought to be indulgence, and indulgence where there ought to be censure." *Mansfield Park* "continually and essentially holds up the vicious as admirable." Austen presents Edmund and Fanny Bertram as not just nice but admirable people. Amis finds them "morally destestable." Austen's not noticing their awfulness "makes *Mansfield Park* an immoral book." The pietistic propriety of the Bertrams is particularly offensive to the attentive reader when Edmund launches puritanical objections to the play *Lovers' Vows,* proposed for a session of private theatricals. He is a pompous prig, and his priggishness Austen approves of. Fanny, on the other hand, is a monster of egotism and self-pity, and worse, she is "disinclined to force herself to be civil to those—a numerous company—whose superior she thinks herself to be." To such emotions as sympathy and pity she is a stranger, and the horror is that Austen's susceptibility to canons of the socially OK has blinded her to Fanny's severe defects. Austen reveals herself to be, in short, a terrible snob, when her reputation is that of a scourge of snobs. What, Amis asks, "became of that Jane Austen (if she ever existed) who set out bravely to correct conventional notions of the desirable and virtuous? From being their critic (if she ever was) she became their slave." Amis grants that there have been "changes in ethical outlook" since her day, but the essential crime of snobbery, despite shifts of costumes and styles, remains an essential crime. Not everyone can see this in Austen, but the boy from Norbury destined to be humiliated at a Cambridge high table can see it clearly. He can see it clearly too because he taught *Mansfield Park* at Swansea, and, as he says, "One never really closes with a work of literature until one has to, e.g., by teaching it, . . . I found out a lot in teaching *Mansfield Park,* but I had concluded that Jane Austen was . . . second rate . . . while still at school." Many of the essays in *What Became of Jane Austen* come equipped with postscripts written in 1970, which sometimes correct and even withdraw Amis's earlier opinions. Not this essay on Austen. It comes close to encapsulating Amis's lifelong views on sympathy for the ordinary person, with its corollary—an author's obligation to anticipate and sympathize with the likely reactions of the reader.

Amis on Keats illustrates another dimension of his courageous willingness to oppose received opinion. Keats's offense, which again only a critic like Amis can see, is bitching about the real world instead of trying to understand it. As he puts it, "If Keats is to be the ideal poet, ideal poetry too readily becomes a tissue of affectionate descriptions of nice things interrupted by occasionial complaints that the real world is insufficiently productive of those nice things." There's a problem too with Keats's favorite style. It is the same tired (as well as implicitly snobbish) neo-classic style reprehended by Johnson in his *Life of Gray* almost forty years before Keats. Johnson had ridiculed Gray's dependence on "the puerilities of obsolete mythology," like "Mars's car and Jove's eagle." Amis finds similar "frigidities" in Keats's "Ode to the Nightingale," like "the blushful Hippocrene (seen as a kind of

Greek red sparkling Burgundy, and apparently sedimented at that)" as well as "Bacchus and his pards (brought in to effect a translation into poetese of the unpoetical notion of getting drunk)." Many of Keats's faults Amis considers the result of impatience with revision—distinctly a moral defect. "Shoddily worked sonnets would be thrown off and dispatched to friends the same day, to reappear unaltered in print." Keats could deal with the real world, as his letters indicate, but the real world "was not the kind of subject that 'a glorious denizen' of Poesy's wide heaven could undertake." These views Amis entertained in 1957. In a postscript of 1970, without altering his opinions on Keats's technical shortcomings, he does admit that he "neglected earlier to celebrate . . . that tremendous originality and audaciousness which went far beyond any mere 'decorative' quality, and, by making poetry personal, so to speak democratized it." Keats's personal "My heart aches" does something genuinely new, enabling "anybody at all to identify with him in the process of reading the poem." *Anybody at all:* there's the Amis keynote.

The general adulation of the poetry of Dylan Thomas makes Amis, in general, quite ill, but in an early encounter with Thomas's work, Amis found in some of his short prose pieces, stories and sketches of actual Welsh life especially, considerable merit, much "humor and truth to fact." But Thomas's whimsy is not always kept at bay, nor is his all-too-famous "verbal free-for-all in which anything whatever may or may not be mentioned. . . ." Thomas's problem was a twentieth-century extension of Keats's: too high-falutin' an idea of "poetry," too little interest in actualities. These reactions come from Amis's review of Thomas's posthumous volume, *A Prospect of the Sea,* edited by one Dr. Daniel Jones. Amis is hard on Jones because Jones seems lazy, his title "editor" flagrantly unearned. Dr. Jones has not told the reader which of these stories has been published before, and where, nor has he bothered to ascertain the accurate texts or even to read the proof carefully. His main labor "would seem to have been that of tearing the stories" out of Thomas's earlier volumes "and sending them off to the printer." But "perhaps it was the toil of arranging the stories in order that earned Dr. Daniel Jones his place on the title-page. After all, if my maths are correct, there were more than 10^{12} combinations to choose from." Worth noting there is Amis's meticulous attention to what he is saying. When an American acquaintance wrote doubting his mathematics, Amis answered in his usual friendly but teacherly epistolary style:

> Ah, but you overlook those two vital words *'more than.'* 10^{12} was a short way of saying one million million: there were I forget how many items in the book, but it was more than 12. I think 18! $>10^{12}$, and 18 isn't so large a number as to make the statement uninteresting.

The Amis attack on snobbery resumes in his essay on his own *Colonel Sun* and on Ian Fleming's James Bond fictions in general: Fleming may have his defects, but "not once, in the twelve books and eight stories, does Bond or his creator come anywhere near judging a character by his or her social standing." There's generic snobbery too to be guarded against. Many of those who denigrate spy fiction, "thrillers," Westerns, ghost stories, horror tales, whodunnits, and other popular narrative forms, are mere snobs affecting (as if instinctive) a socially advantageous leaning towards "serious fiction" and other manifestations of high culture. But actually, Amis is brave enough to say right out loud, "John D. MacDonald is by any standards a better writer than Saul Bellow."

If that sort of remark is bound to offend certain academics who conceive that any poem by, say Arthur Hugh Clough is better than any tale by, say, Sir Arthur Conan Doyle, Amis's essay on *Lolita* is bound to offend, as it did offend, almost everyone else. Amis dislikes *Lolita* intensely, and it is by no means its sexiness that bothers him. Indeed, one of its faults is its failure to convey significant details of Humbert's lovemaking and thus gratify a normal reader's curiosity. Thus, "one of the troubles with *Lolita* is that, so far from being too pornographic, it is not pornographic enough." No, what annoys him is not moral but artistic, or if moral, then moral in a way bad art is ipso facto immoral. This wouldn't matter so much if the book had not been heralded as a rare masterpiece, inviting a cascade of honorific critical language from its champions and blurb-writers—*distinguished, brilliant, great, major, masterpiece.* The book has arrived in Britain "preceded by a sort of creeping barrage of critical acclaim," prompting, in Amis, first wonderment, then indignation.

What's immoral about *Lolita* is, first of all, the style, which despite Nabokov's maintaining that it is Humbert's, not his, is by comparison with Nabokov's other writing clearly Nabokov's own. It is a style full of gestures betraying self-concern in the author and a high level of personal vanity. The reader's attention to the human situation is constantly distracted by "the sustained din of pun, allusion, neologism, alliteration, . . . apostrophe, parenthesis, rhetorical question, French, Latin, 'anent,' 'perchance,' 'would fain,' 'for the nonce,'—here is style and no mistake." "This is Nabokov talking," Amis insists, this is "émigré's euphuism." As Amis says elsewhere, "Nabokov, in a way peculiar to foreigners, never stops showing off his mastery of the language; his books are jewels a hundred thousand words long." And he still hasn't managed to avoid solecisms and vulgar errors inappropriate to his pretensions. "Mr. Chamberlain literally bubbled over with gratitude," he will write, and "with his eyes he literally scoured the corners of the cell." If he means *virtually,* why not say so?

But the show-off style is not the only evidence of immorality. Perhaps more telling is the cruelty, not at all essential to the narrative, thrown in, as it were, for pure entertainment. Some of this can be imputed to Humbert, "but the many totally incidental cruelties—the bloody car wreck by the roadside that brings into view the kind of shoe Lolita covets, the wounding of a squirrel, apparently just for fun—bring the author into consideration as well, and I really don't care which of them is being wonderfully mature and devastating when Lolita's mother (recently Humbert's wife) is run over and killed." Here Nabokov goes into a flurry of stylistic exhibitionism as he describes what the dead woman's head looked like: the top of her head was "a porridge of bone, brains, bronze hair and blood." Amis comments: "That's the boy, Humbert/Nabokov: alliterative to the last." The critic speaking there is the author of *The Anti-Death League*, abnormally sensitive to the pain and injustice that rule the world, a fact calling for tears, not displays of wit.

On the other hand, loathsome as elements of *Lolita* are, Amis tries to be fair by honestly registering the effect on him of some very telling descriptive moments constituting "the portrait of Lolita herself." He says, "I have rarely seen the external ambience of a character so marvellously realized, and yet there is seldom more than the necessary undertone of sensuality." But finally the girl Lolita "is a portrait in a very full sense, devotedly watched and listened to but never conversed with, the object of desire but never of curiosity. What did she do in Humbert's presence but play tennis and eat sundaes and go to bed with him? What did they talk about?" To the melodrama and farce of *Lolita* Amis vastly prefers Nabokov's seven-page story "Colette," published in 1948, where "the Biarritz world of pre-1914 is evoked with a tender intensity" absent from *Lolita*. "Colette" is also about a lost love, but there the theme is treated with an appropriate, and human, tenderness, remorse, and subtlety, with no jokes and no hokey alliteration:

> Instantly she was off, tap-tapping her glinting hoop through light and shade, around and around a fountain choked with dead leaves, near which I stood. The leaves mingled in my memory with the leather of her shoes and gloves, and there was, I remember, some detail in her attire (perhaps a ribbon on her Scottish cap, or the pattern of her stockings) that reminded me then of the rainbow spiral in a glass marble. I still seem to be holding that wisp of iridescence, not knowing exactly where to fit it in, while she runs with her hoop ever faster around me and finally dissolves among the slender shadows cast on the gravelled path by the interlaced arches of its border.

Amis's ability to look at both sides, as when he does not allow himself, in his annoyance, to overlook the delightful, artistically successful bits in *Lolita,* is at work too in his essay on Richard Hoggart's examination of the British working class, *The Uses of Literacy* (1957), where Amis reveals that his knowledge of people of this class is deep, detailed, and sympathetic. Some of Hoggart's portraits of women, "the wife endlessly working to keep the household warm, properly fed and out of debt, the widow struggling to bring up three or four young children"—"and the various evocations of Friday-evening shopping or Sunday-morning leisure, distil a warmth that cannot fail to engage sympathy." But the other side must be looked at, too, a side Hoggart skimps, namely "characteristic proletarian vices." Like "the serene intolerant complacency manifested by many working-class people, especially older women; the skin-tight armor against any unfamiliar idea." And yet, what can one feel but sorrow and anger watching the way these people are treated by officials (*"Want's* your portion!")? Social workers and the like who read Hoggart's book "will find grounds for exercising the utmost kindness and patience in their dealings."

Readers accustomed to Amis's frequent sneers at Americans, especially academics with their ignorance, clumsiness, and illiteracy, may be surprised by his views on Leslie Fiedler and his *Love and Death in the American Novel* (1961). As a literary person to be taken seriously, Fiedler would seem to have, from Amis's view, everything against him. The photograph on the jacket depicts someone very like a superannuated beatnik, facial hair and all, and seems to call for "a background a row of bottles rather than of Oxford texts." But appearance aside, there's something about Fiedler's performance in this book that rapidly wins Amis's admiration. It is Fiedler's energy and brilliance and risk-taking, and Amis is happy to admit that few in England would be original enough to attempt bold and imaginative criticism of this kind. "There is something striking—and American—in the mere readiness to attempt a work of this size and scope on such a high level of scholarship and intelligence." Fiedler's main point is by now too well known to need much elucidation: American fiction, he has noticed, is sadly deficient in works dissecting and interpreting the kind of man-woman love the art of the rest of the world likes to deal with, like Tolstoy, Balzac, Hardy, or Conrad. Classic American fiction (which means fiction largely of the nineteenth century), on the contrary, is rich in "Platonic" love affairs, or quasi-love affairs, or disguised, or aborted love-affairs, between men, or between a man and a boy, or between a "white" man or boy and a "colored" one. Natty Bumppo and Chingachgook, Ishmael and Queequeg, Jim and Huck are Fiedler's main examples, and Amis, immediately taken with the idea, adds the Lone Ranger and Tonto. In contemplating this audacious and brilliant formulation, Amis confesses to being impressed by Fiedler's "tact and seriousness." He is concerned, Amis notes, "not to shock or titillate but to explain." If he does often "go too far," it is frequently in "a new and illuminating direction." Amis is happy to play quite along with Fiedler's evident pleasure in multiplying examples, as when Fiedler focuses on the Gothic impulse in American fiction, with its fixation on horror and fantasy and perverse sensationalism (Poe, Hawthorne, Faulkner), and Amis quickly makes his own contribution, "Alfred Hitchcock's *Psycho*, that incredible salad of demoniacal possession, transvestism, incest, and necrophily, with the obligatory miasmic swamp in the background." *Psycho*, Amis goes on, makes "British-made chillers like *Dracula* seem chronicles of harmless eccentricity." Despite a few moments of wild excess, Fiedler's "witty, exasperating, energetic, penetrating book will prove indispensable" for anyone interested in national characteristics as reflected in art. As well as, Amis implies, setting an example for the British of how absorbing and stimulating literary history and criticism can be in bold and ungenteel hands.

Like *Lolita*, another wildly popular and critically celebrated book which left Amis cold is Philip Roth's *Portnoy's Complaint*. "Jewish jokes are not funny," he begins, and they are not funny because the humor is in collusion with too much melancholy and anger, the result of racial abuse by a world which regards those without social success and even conventional good looks as contemptible. Victimization implies victimizers, victimizers imply cruelty, and cruelty is not to be dealt with by the guffaws occasioned by the comic novel. Roth's book, Amis acknowledges, is "fluent, lively, articulate, vivid, energetic—all that and more; but as the stream of Jewish-joke-type incidents and epigrams and soliloquies thickened, I found myself hankering for some variation, . . . a bit of farce of a comic line at which one was not invited to laugh once and cry twice and gag three times and rage four times." (In a later footnote, he indicates that on second or third thought, he'd like to withdraw all the attractive characteristics of *Portnoy's Complaint* he originally listed except *fluent*.)

And again, as with *Lolita*, it's not the sexual theme and here, the precise sexual detail, that Amis objects to. Indeed, he rather admires Roth's clearly autobiographical honesty as well as his suggestion that such excessive masturbation as Portnoy's may stem from "resentment at continual parental presence" and nosiness. No, Amis's real objection to this novel is that it's not a novel. It's a collection of sketches, clumsily seamed together as if to hoodwink the consumer into thinking that he's reading something else, and something else much harder to do. The book is made of "odd scraps," a point that becomes all too clear when the reader consults the back of the title-page and finds that "Sections of this book have appeared in slightly different form" in several classy periodicals. "The magazine," Amis concludes, "is the enemy of the novel," and this seems especially an American hazard. "We in England are lucky to have no counterparts [of these magazines], no temptations, no arrangements, to send in whatever we are working on as soon as it gets to thirty or forty pages." Regardless of the cause, however, *Portnoy's Complaint* "is not a narrative, not simply in that it is incoherent, but in that the commentary swamps, erodes, and drowns out character and incident." And furthermore, it seems too merely autobiographical—one indication being the disappearance from the plot of Portnoy's woman, "the Monkey," once she's served her largely pornographic purpose. It's all too much about Roth's own life: "Mr. Roth's unconcern to narrate is connected with his unconcern to invent." Amis isn't quite sure that he's right

77

here, that Roth hasn't simply made this all up, but he's willing to risk being wrong. Roth's subsequent production, since 1969, shows how right Amis's instincts were. He sensed not only the truth but hinted at the obsession in Roth that, in the view of many, has restricted his range and even prevented him from growing into the major writer he might have become.

Literal-mindedness and a want of invention pose threats to writing elsewhere. The focus of Amis's essay "Unreal Policemen" is the traditional intellectual attributes of the great detectives in the classic narratives by Conan Doyle, Simenon, Chesterton, Rex Stout, and John Dickson Carr. "All the sleuths we remember and reverence and take into our private pantheon of heroes," he says, "are figures not of realism but of fantasy, great talkers, great eccentrics, men who use inspiration more than hard work, men to whom Venetian old masters mean more than police files and a good bottle of Burgundy more than fingerprints." By their ability to solve riddles and puzzles, these detectives implicitly celebrate "the power of the human mind to observe and to reason." But what's happened? About 1950 this kind of classic detective vanished, and so did "the classical detective story, in which all the clues were scrupulously put before the reader." That intellectual hero has been replaced by the real policeman, as well as the secret agent, the international spy, and the tough operative whose muscle and cynicism make up for his defect of brain. For confirmation, go into any popular bookstore and observe the new classification, True Crime. Who wants fiction and art and mind when actuality is so easily available?

Amis rounds off *What Became of Jane Austen* with an essay on the conventions of horror films, and with some autobiographical pieces later retrieved for the *Memoirs,* together with his attack on the uncritical expansion of the universities in the 1960s. Here, his memorable words "More Will Mean Worse" became notorious, even if true. "University graduates," he explains, and he means real university graduates, not current-events specialists or business-school products, "are like poems or bottles of hock, and unlike cars or tins of salmon, in that you cannot *decide* to have more good ones." The threat to genuine learning is from all sorts of "quantitative thinkers," as well as from those who conceive the function of the university to create not analyzers and critics and doubters but docile members of a society whose greatest cultural invention is advertising. Amis gave further offense to progressives and utilitarians by asserting that the university, like the church, "must shut her mind firmly against the needs of society," and like the church, "this is not only her age-old duty, it is also her only chance of turning out in the end to have served the needs of society."

This is conservative stuff, surely, to be understood in part by the illumination cast by the essay "Why Lucky Jim Turned Right." Why did Amis turn to the Right? Because he's always been uneasy with orthodoxy, as well as with pretension, self-righteousness, and humorlessness. If the phonies used to be on the Right, they are now found largely on the Left, and after Amis had noticed how few on the Left seemed much bothered by the Russian military intervention into Hungarian affairs, he began to see the light. It was authoritarianism in any form that he came to see as the enemy, and it was his devotion to absolute freedom of utterance that made him hate communism and its liberal apologists with a vengeance. His liberation from the orthodoxy of the Left will surprise few familiar with his liberation from the orthodoxy of artistic Modernism. In both, Big Brother tells the ordinary person what he should approve of.

Another orthodoxy is the religious one, and here Amis mounts a thoughtful attack in his final essay, "On Christ's Nature." Christ is an impressive generator of moral paradoxes, all right, and his values—as in the model of the Good Samaritan—are admirable. His selecting as companions and followers men largely from the working class is greatly to his credit. But the problem for a civilized searcher after religious illumination is Christ's proclaimed loyalty to a God Amis finds loathsome in every way. Amis's religious thought is rough and ready, with little tolerance for theological niceties. He declines to be fancy or over-subtle about the problem of evil, and he declines to revere a God who has seen to it that his universe allows the innocent to suffer, merit to go unrewarded, and scourges like cancer and deformity to torment the harmless and the good. Thus, "in rough proportion as he moves away from being divine Jesus invites approval and affection," but "God" is another question altogether. The Russian poet Yevgeny Yevtushenko once asked Amis, "You atheist?" Amis answered, "Well, yes, but it's more that I hate him." And it's not just God's cruelty that bothers Amis. It's his prescriptive authoritarianism, suggestive more of a dotty sadistic commissar than a heavenly father one loves and respects. Given Amis's opposition to coercion, given his ready sympathy with the deprived and unfortunate, his views on God and Christ follow naturally and become an indispensable element in his outlook and his criticism.

In 1990 he published a second gathering of non-fiction pieces, *The Amis Collection,* in which he recovered about half his miscellaneous writings, many from the *Observer* and the *Spectator,* from the previous thirty years. This volume, almost twice as long as *Jane Austen,* contains a greater variety of things: comments about writing in general and advice to beginners; critical assessments of authors; comments on anthologies and suggestions for their proper conduct; essays on society and education; observations on language; and brief treatments of film, travel, and music. And of course a section on "Eating and Drinking."

Literary egotism being one of Amis's special aversions, it's hardly a surprise to find the lead essay in the book returning to what can be called the *Portnoy Fallacy,* whose first practitioner was probably D. H. Lawrence. This is the novelist's erroneous assumption that writing about things that have happened to him and to real people he has known will guarantee greater authenticity and verisimilitude than writing about made-up events and people. But what this practice actually does is to lull the author into complacency about how well he's doing. Because events from his past seem "real" and gripping and fascinating to him, what reason is there to suppose that they're going to work that way with the reader? It's useful here to notice that most writers' first novels are really autobiographies in disguise, and that (as publishers know) they are for that reason very likely to be bad novels. That view is what lies behind Amis's praise of Iris Murdoch's *Under the Net* as a valuable rarity, "a thoroughly accomplished first novel." Focusing on oneself, delightful though that process admittedly is, is an almost sure-fire way to avoid the crucial, perhaps the only literary question, how is this bit of writing going to go down with strangers?

Karl Miller is one who has noticed without much pleasure Amis's habit in his fiction of placing offensive social opinions that are really his own in the mouths of unsavory characters, like Patrick Standish, Roger Micheldene, Ronnie Appleyard, or Alun Weaver. To Miller, this seems like an attempt to have it both ways, to utter nasty views while appearing to disown them. But Amis's interpretation is quite different. The novelist's central characters, he admits, are and are not the novelist, but the intent is less to distance the author, cunningly, from vile opinions he really holds than to engage in an act of self-criticism:

> The novelist's . . . central characters are clearly meant to do more than just go around being close or distant relatives of him. . . . They are vehicles of his self-criticism. . . . By that very act of distancing, by projecting himself into an entity that is part of himself and yet not himself, he may be able to see more clearly, and judge more harshly, his own weaknesses and follies; and, since he must know that no failings are unique, he may be helped to acquire tolerance for them in others. [And] if the novel comes off at all, the reader will perhaps accompany the writer in some parallel process of self-discovery.

Not everyone will be convinced by this: Amis's pleasure in voicing unfashionable offensive views is so evident that the subject of *pleasure,* as well as *moral duty,* deserves a look-in too. Something besides a noble self-flagellation seems to be going on.

In several essays in *The Amis Collection* he considers a recurring topic, the defects of American writing, and concludes that a large part of the problem is the American writers' and critics' "pursuit of the masterpiece." He has kind words for Whitman and the Salinger of *The Catcher in the Rye* ("marvellous"), but observes that America, still anxious for a distinguished culture all her own, "takes her writers too seriously." The result is pretentiousness and an urge to hypertrophy, producing a succession of overweight flops, usually one per season. More modesty is what's wanted, more understanding that the "minor" writer is not for that reason a failure.

To Amis, some Americans, like some academics, are nothing less than awful. The two are handily available for a sound drubbing in the figure of Professor Hugh Kenner, of the Johns Hopkins University. The theme of his book on modern British literary achievement is right there in its title, *The Sinking Island: The Modern English Writers* (1988). Kenner, "a veteran American critic and teacher," is well known as an enthusiastic celebrator of "International Modernism" as illustrated pre-eminently in the works of Pound, Wyndham Lewis, Eliot, and Joyce, on all of whom he's written copiously. The argument of this book is that "Modernism" was brought about largely by the Americans and the Irish, with minimal help, or even understanding, from the English. Fair enough, perhaps, if you think literature and general culture improved by the spirit of "International Modernism." Amis does not, observing that the Modernist movement has alienated the general reader from serious writing and has allowed him, by default, to drift away to the films, the television, and the football stadium. "Dr. Kenner reveals . . . his whole literary position, when he characterizes *The Waste Land* as above all 'the century's most influential poem' and a 'supremely important poem.' If you see literature as a matter of influences and importances *of course* you are going to fall for International Modernism with its innovativeness, experiments, developments and echoes, so much more inviting to lecture on than the intractable, unclassifiable qualities of an actual work of literature. . . . Importance isn't important. Only good writing is." Speaking of which, Amis does not scruple to impugn Kenner's prose as well as his views, imputing to it specifically

American academic faults, like careless diction (the result of pretentiousness and the quest for novelty)—for example, Kenner's saying of Aubrey Beardsley's "sense of line and design" that it is *irrefutable,* or finding it *orienting* that Everyman's Library followed the death of Samuel Johnson by only 65 years. Amis the critic speaks in this essay, but audible also is Amis the patriot—with his back up.

Two essays in *The Amis Collection* celebrate the unpretentious virtues of the publisher Victor Gollancz, who issued excellent books from a shabby office devoid of "oak panelling, sporting print and sherry decanter." He was Amis's publisher for five of his novels, from *Lucky Jim* in 1954 to *One Fat Englishman* in 1963. Gollancz was an example of *"unconscious* goodness," and although a "monster of egotism, vanity and self-delusion . . . [he] was also entirely capable of disinterested generosity both moral and monetary, genuine warmth of heart and readiness to go to endless trouble on behalf of those he valued." His nose for the market as well as his sense of quality can be suggested by his publishing Shaw and Orwell, as well as Amis. His Left Book Club enrolled 57,000 subscribers in 1939 and it doubtless assisted the victory of the Labour Party in 1945. He had an extraordinary talent for spotting winners. When he saw R. C. Sherriff's *Journey's End* he indicated at the first intermission that he'd be delighted to publish it. If he hurled himself too uncritically into socialist causes and thought too highly of the USSR, Amis seems ready to forgive him, for he published and encouraged Amis when no one had heard of him.

Almost a third of *The Amis Collection* is devoted to essays on such novelists as Iris Murdoch, Anthony Powell, Orwell, Somerset Maugham, Evelyn Waugh, Angus Wilson, Anthony Burgess, and William Golding, together with such lesser-known Amis favorites as Elizabeth Taylor and William Cooper (*Scenes from Provincial Life,* 1950), and a handful of science-fiction and detective-story worthies. There are also essays on such people of letters as Max Beerbohm, Kipling, Chesterton, Quiller-Couch, C. S. Lewis, William Empson, the boys' writer "Frank Richards," A. Conan

Doyle, and Julian Symons. Such Yanks as Poe and Ambrose Bierce are also passed under inspection. He's written here on the lives and works of poets too: Browning, Tennyson, Swinburne, Housman, Wilfred Owen, Robert Graves, Dylan Thomas, and Philip Larkin. And he's talked about the author or authors of *Beowulf*, whoever they may be, candidates for the distinction, together with the perpetrators of *Piers Plowman* and *Sir Gawain and the Green Knight*, of creating the most boring poem in Old, Middle, or Modern English.

Max Beerbohm has been acclaimed so incontinently by such as Lord David Cecil and E. M. Forster that he must be cut down a bit. One reason is that terrible people refer to him as "Max." Indeed, any author known by his or her first name ("Jane," "Emily") is very likely to be admired by people Amis cannot bring himself to like. How did it happen, he wonders, that "it ever got about in the first place that he [Beerbohm] was worth taking seriously?" Actually, he has nothing to say, his whole stock in trade being "style." And as a critic, Beerbohm is habitually ungenerous, hardly ever avoiding "a note of coldness and disparagement." A sort of proto-Cyril Connolly, Beerbohm was obsessed with "failure, with setting one's aim safely low." His parodies of H. G. Wells, Henry James, and Kipling, as well as his cartoons, are lively and funny, but his alleged masterpiece, *Zuleika Dobson*, remains for Amis a silly, camp, self-consciously cute book implicitly recommending everything at Oxford that is superficial, shallow, and stupid. That novel merely prolongs the insidious belief that Oxford is a place less of scholarship than of magic social prestige and general faerie.

That makes Beerbohm sound almost like the aged Evelyn Waugh, glorifying all the repulsive things about the rich and their clubs, including "exclusive" old-fashioned religions and antique military regiments. Amis's fascination with the final perversion of Waugh's career by snobbery is so intense that he devotes more pages to him than to any other writer. And it's not just snobbery. Amis likewise presents Waugh as an example of the way literature can be ruined, or at least badly weakened, by the intrusion of things that are not literature—in Waugh's case, religion, self-righteousness, and irrelevant anger. *Decline and Fall* and *A Handful of Dust* Amis is happy to praise as successful farces on the theme of "the cruelty and arbitrariness at the heart of the universe." Waugh's depression on this score gradually propelled him in the direction of a system offering an explanation, or a palliative, or something like them. He thus embraced Catholicism, but "to his artistic detriment," and what before had been "an enlivening bitterness" came forth now as "defiance and jeering," together with an embarrassing conviction of personal superiority. The sense of humor hardened into a sense of *I* and *Thou*, with the *I* always right and admirable.

The damage, Amis notes, is abundantly available for contemplation in the *Sword of Honor* trilogy, where Waugh seems to have no idea how repulsive he's made the self-righteous Catholic Guy Crouchback. And Waugh's view of army life is also troubling. It is unsatisfyingly ambiguous and at bottom unsatiric, indeed, admiring. "If one is really going to satirize army life," says Amis, "in all its confusion and arbitrariness, then sooner or later one has got to start satirizing the army itself, which contains in its nature confusion and arbitrariness just as much as order and custom." But Waugh can't satirize the army effectively because he really believes in it too much. It would be like satirizing the Catholic Church. He slavers over Crouchback's regiment just as he does over the church, and for similar reasons, its antiquity, oddity, ceremonial obsession, and airs of superiority. Like the regiment, you don't just "join" the church as if it were a mere social organization. You are "received" into it. "Crouchback is really a terrible fellow," Amis concludes, basing much of this view on the scene "where he tries to seduce his ex-wife in the flush of the discovery that theologically he would be committing no sin." Waugh seems less ready than the reader to agree at that point with the wife, who addresses Guy with, as Amis notes, "truth and finality": "You wet, smug, obscene, pompous, sexless lunatic pig."

Waugh seems equally insensitive to a reader's natural response to Crouchback's prolonged search for an army assignment presumably appropriate to his talents, his social standing, and his own opinion of his value. Very early in the war he's to be found nosing around London in search of a job in the service, and of course he must have a commission. He seeks out "powerful friends at Bellamy's" and writes begging letters to "Cabinet ministers' wives." Contemplating this behavior, unrebuked by its creator and delineator, Amis flies into a democratic fury, asking, "What about all those jobs in the ranks . . . ?—Unthinkable, naturally," for someone like Crouchback. After all, what's the use of powerful friends from school and university if they can't get you made a captain even though you have neither knowledge, talent, or training? The terrible truth, and Amis oddly refrains from coming right out with it, is that Crouchback *is* Waugh and is therefore, to his author and admirer, largely beyond criticism. Or even analysis.

But one must go to *Brideshead Revisited,* both the novel and the lush TV enactment, to witness the worst. There, as Amis puts it, "Waugh's snobbery rages unchecked . . . by the habitual austerities of his style." A reader of "this bad book" would be justified in believing that "since about all [Waugh] looked for in his companions was wealth, rank, Roman Catholicism (where possible) and beauty (where appropriate), those same attributes and no more would be sufficient for the central characters in a long novel . . . to establish them as both glamorous and morally significant." Here Waugh treats such characters "with an almost cringing respect," producing a work Amis "would rather expect a conscientious Catholic to find repulsive" for its yoking of the True Faith with unearned money, social privilege, immense, richly furnished premises, and the very best in food, drink, and servants. No one at Brideshead is a better person for being a Catholic. Merely more self-satisfied. As Waugh's biographer Martin Stannard points out, Waugh, annoyed by Amis's views when they appeared in the *Spectator,* wanted to impute Amis's response to his presumed lower-class origins and, as a new aspirant comic novelist, to mere jealousy of Waugh's earlier success in this mode. He of course did not understand the full weight of Amis's moral disapproval, or notice that the essence of Amis's attack involved a compliment, and regret at a terrible loss. What Amis was registering was, as Stannard says, "disappointment . . . at Waugh's continued suppression of 'that farcical vein which founded his reputation'."

Getting in a final lick at Poe ("Before he turned up, there had been plenty of writers who were no good—Herrick, Cowley, Cowper; Poe's distinction is to have been the first who was positively bad"), Amis turns to the poets. He pauses for some time over Tennyson and does what perhaps he does best as a critic. He confronts "a massive prejudice" against a given writer (Kipling, Newbolt, Betjeman) and tries to argue his detractors into a new kind of, if not acceptance, at least reconsideration and tolerance. Amis sees Tennyson as a brilliant, original, instinctive poet when young, but one gradually pre-empted by the more genteel elements of his world "to become in time a figure uncomfortably close to that pensioner of the establishment taken by many . . . to be all he had ever been." In hostile folklore, Tennyson ends reading his works to his Sovereign (Beerbohm's cartoon is unforgettable) and, no doubt in consequence, receiving the Laurel. As a result of his close friend Arthur Henry Hallam's death at the age of twenty-two, Tennyson learned to register sorrow and loss like almost no other writer of his time—until, perhaps, Housman, and later still, perhaps, Amis. And not just sorrow and loss but "the feelings that lie close to it, despondency, ennui, nostalgia, loneliness, despair and the desire for reconciliation and resignation."

After judicious treatment of Housman and Wilfred Owen and Robert Graves, Amis arrives at the task of dealing with three books which invite the sternest moral (and critical) disapproval of Dylan Thomas. The first is Paul Ferris's biography, which specifies that Thomas was "a chronic liar," sponger, and draft-dodger, overflowing with self-pity, a man who apparently conceived that his talent justified his non-payment of bills presented by tradesmen and landlords. He and his wife Caitlin were given to simply showing up at friends' houses at night, bedding down for weeks, and then stealing the silver. He was a monumental drinker, but also liked to lie about the number of drinks he'd put down. Playing the poet, in the adolescent, Romantic sense of that word, was more important to him than producing poems. He knew but did not advertise the fact that after about the age of twenty, he wrote nothing worth reading. Copious evidence of his shortcomings is available also in Ferris's edition of Thomas's *Collected Letters.* He proclaimed his need for utter independence—from, say, a regular job—but ironically fell into greater dependence thereby, since one spends all one's time managing one's mendicancy, composing begging letters, and contriving lies. Thomas's poetic subject was his childhood, and he did quite well there. But once childhood had passed, "he had nothing more to write about because he had noticed nothing since." His letters "show no curiosity about other people or their lives," as well as suggesting that he read little and was not very interested in literature. (He could have stolen books, but apparently didn't care to.) The third book, *Caitlin: Life with Dylan Thomas,* by his wife with the aid of George Tremlett, serves, unwittingly, to blacken her character too. Despite vivid public quarrels, "what held them together was devotion not only to booze but also to petty criminality, minor fraud, stealing from friends, and messing up their houses, cheating, cadging, above all a shared conviction that rich, complacent people, i.e., those living on their own earnings, deserved to have anything movable taken off them by footloose creative souls like Mr. and Mrs. Dylan Thomas."

Philip Larkin's life and works, to which Amis turns now, make a contrast perhaps too melodramatic. Amis notes his admiration and pleasure at encountering the volume *High Windows* for the first time. Larkin finds his perfect reader in Amis, whose taste is sure for what is best in Larkin's work. Of course he admires "To the Sea" and "Show Saturday," not just because they evoke the pleasure ordinary people take in simple, permanent things, but because of their unshowy art, especially the way their rhymes are so exquisitely managed that the reader is likely not to notice that he is reading a rhyming poem until asking, "What's holding this all together?" Here's the way "To the Sea" begins:

> To step over the low wall that divides
> Road from concrete walk above the shore
> Brings sharply back something known long before—
> The miniature gaiety of seasides.
> Everything crowds under the low horizon:
> Steep beach, blue water, towels, red bathing caps,
> The small hushed waves' repeated fresh collapse
> Up the warm yellow sand, and further off
> A white steamer stuck in the afternoon—
>
> Still going on, all of it, still going on!
> To lie, eat, sleep in hearing of the surf
> (Ears to transistors, that sound tame enough
> Under the sky), or gently up and down
> Lead the uncertain children, frilled in white
> And grasping at enormous air, or wheel
> The rigid old along for them to feel
> A final summer, plainly still occurs
> As half an annual pleasure, half a rite.

The day beginning to end,

>   the first
> Few families start the trek back to the cars.
> The white steamer has gone. Like breathed-on glass
> The sunlight has turned milky. If the worst
> Of flawless weather is our falling short,
> It may be that through habit these do best,
> Coming to water clumsily undressed
> Yearly; teaching their children by a sort
> Of clowning; helping the old, too, as they ought.

That's Betjeman (or even Blunden) raised to the highest power. The same sort of understanding of permanent rituals distinguishes "Show Saturday," about a country fair combining judging of live-stock, display of homemade foodstuffs,

> a beer-marquee
> That half-screens a canvas Gents; a tent selling tweed,
> And another, jackets,

as well as

> Needlework, knitted caps, baskets, all worthy, all well done.

But it has to end, and the fair folds up, the crowds disperse and go home:

> Back now, all of them, to their local lives:
> To names on vans, and business calendars
> Hung up in kitchens; back to loud occasions
> In the Corn exchange, to market days in bars,
>
> To winter coming, as the dismantled Show
> Itself dies back into the area of work.
> Let it stay hidden there like strength, below
> Sale-bills and swindling; something people do,
> Not noticing how time's rolling smithy-smoke
> Shadows much greater gestures; something they share
> That breaks ancestrally each year into
> Regenerate union. Let it always be there.

That helps show why Amis is Larkin's greatest fan and champion, and it illustrates something more. It helps suggest why Modernism has had so much trouble domesticating itself in England, whose possession of that solid, almost unitary, local descriptive, quasi-pastoral vision and technique is firm and satisfying enough for its performers and readers to feel no need for a revolution.

Amis is skilled enough in Larkin's procedures to sense that "At Grass" is the first poem in the mode Larkin made his own. "It seems almost suddenly that he learnt to take his images from the world of reality and show us, in the vividly drawn picture of a pair of old racehorses, the evanescence of glory, of active life and of life itself." Now quite retired and hidden away from crowds and cheering, the two horses

> . . . gallop for what must be joy,
> And not a fieldglass sees them home,
> Or curious stop-watch prophesies:
> Only the groom, and the groom's boy,
> With bridles in the evening come.

There's the elegiac note that seems curiously English and that Amis responds to so readily and so emotionally. Given Larkin's good luck in attracting Amis as a critic, it's tiresome to see quoted, in George Hartley's book of tributes to Larkin and critical essays on his work, silly, pretentious, mechanical workouts like, for example, Steve Clark's. He specializes in clumsy application of irrelevant aperçus of Freud and Derrida to a poetry quite whole and complete without that kind of make-work. As Larkin once said, "There's not much to say about my work. When you've read a poem, that's it, it's all quite clear what it means." And before leaving the topic of Larkin and his frustrated explicators, Amis takes one more swipe at a professor, this one a hapless Canadian (always, it seems, fair game) whose brash misquotations of Larkin's lines screw up the meter and betray the critic's lack of fitness "to write a book on any subject of this sort." A professor of English need not be bright, but he/she should care enough about words to refrain from offering as Milton's the line,

> They serve also who stand and wait.

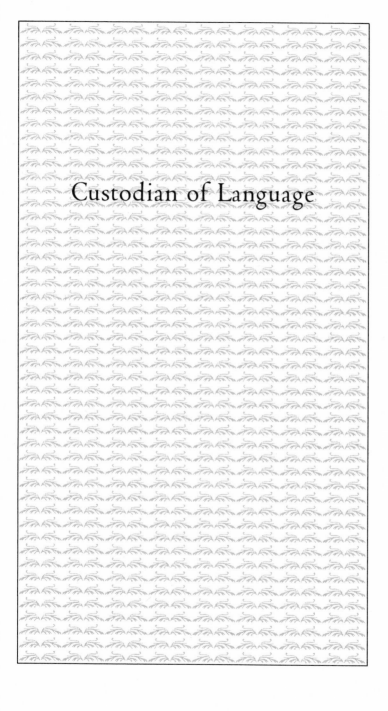

Custodian of Language

MEMBERS of that small minority who care about the use of words," Amis writes, "are likely to be dismayed, or outraged, or infuriated every time they open a newspaper or a periodical and nearly every time they open a contemporary novel." Actually, one of today's rarest things is a novelist who is a master of his/her medium—words —and profoundly interested in their tones, colors, sounds, echoes, histories, and complexities and who shuns clichés—like the plague. Amis is such a novelist, and so in his way is Anthony Burgess, although his relations with language seem, next to Amis's, nervous, not at all assured, with the linguistic autodidact's obsession with etymology, which, rather than usage and context, Burgess tends to confuse with meaning. Lady Kilmarnock, formerly Hilly Bardwell Amis, recalls that when she and Amis were getting acquainted at Oxford, he always carried a dictionary. "I knew from the start," she says, "that this man would teach me a lot."

As many have noted, Amis tends to write as if the eye of early Evelyn Waugh were on him. In 1946 Waugh declared,

> When I gadded among savages and people of fashion and politicians and crazy generals, it was because I enjoyed them. I have found a much more abiding interest—the English language. . . . It is the most lavish and delicate which mankind has ever known. It is in perpetual danger of extinction and has survived so far by the combination of a highly civilized society, where it was

spoken and given its authority and sanctity, with a thin line of devotees who make its refinement and adornment their life's work.

Except for the high-society note here, there's little that Amis couldn't subscribe to, and Waugh's own style Amis has designated "an elegant instrument based on scrupulous attention to syntax and word order." I have noted before Amis's devotion to language and extraordinarily high respect for it, not just in writing but in conversation. In nearly forty years of acquaintanceship, I have never heard him come close to misusing a word or failing to catch a solecism, or even a bad rhythm, in writing or speaking. He takes these things so seriously, indeed, that friendship confers no immunity against vigorous, even teacherly, correction. He has rebuked me in writing for my use of *perceive* and *perception* as virtual synonyms for *observe* or *seeing* rather than indications of one's penetration into absolute, objective truth.

His preoccupation with words properly and productively used appears everywhere, even, for example, in the most trivial word games. He used to play with his sons, and finally with me and other friends, a game which might be called Professional Anagrams. The object was to contrive an appropriate name for the practitioner of an out-of-the-way profession, deriving all the letters of the one from the other. The model was Canon Victor Lopes, the Portuguese cleric lucky enough to have been appointed for life a *Volcano Inspector.* Others that delighted Amis were Terence Stag (*Secret Agent*) and Señor Mathias C. Prudente (*South-American President*). Silly as that exercise is, it does register Amis's simultaneous pleasure in words, people, and the work of the imagination—indispensable concerns for the novelist. (Ironically, it was his admiration for Leo Rosten's management of language in the Hyman Kaplan stories that seduced him into violating one of his firm principles: never accept a stranger's invitation to dinner. Drinks, perhaps, but never dinner.)

It's his interest in language as an index of character that makes him a novelist who likes to begin a narrative with a sentence—

often rudely interrupted—spoken by one of the characters. The first words of *Lucky Jim* are "They made a silly mistake, though," spoken by Professor Welch, and of *The Old Devils,* "If you want my opinion," from Gwen Cellan-Davies. He has said that he finds dialogue "relatively easy" to write, and "everything else arduous." And as Karl Miller and many others have noticed, Amis's elevated standards of eloquence make him unable to resist imputing something like rhetorical distinction to all his characters, no matter how low or unlikely. (His senior NCOs are an example.) In an age of moral waffling, he is courageous enough to retain the concept "bad people" and, when necessary, to write it. "Nothing gives bad people away," he declares, "like what they say and write." Pretentious illiteracy—how about "In regards to?"—is to him not just a mark of the unfortunate but a sign of "the wicked." Hence his lifelong fascination with English usage and the way it reveals character and moral status.

Wilson Follett and Jacques Barzun's *Modern American Usage* (1966) he designates "a sustained, ferocious and above all witty assault on an enormous range of linguistic barbarity." And although the focus is on American carelessness and pretentiousness, the British reader can take away much too. The book "pricks our own complacency: I, for one, will not again write 'represents' when I mean 'is'." But the true usefulness of the book "is to serve as a lasting reminder of the need for continuous self-criticism on the part of any writer. The price of good style is eternal vigilance."

One of Amis's minor, harmless obsessions is his belief that Americans are especially puritanical and that their language comically betrays this fact. They have, he is convinced, contrived a whole closetful of euphemisms to avoid any suggestions of obscenity, lubricity, or indelicate anatomical designation. Thus, he finds, Americans prefer *rooster* to *cock, roach* to *cockroach.* Since *bag* once betokened *scrotum,* Americans, he asserts, avoid the possible indelicate ambiguity with *paper sack.* For the same reason, they say *handbag* to avoid *purse.* Puritanism turns British *titbit* to American *tidbit.* All perhaps close to the mark. But when he imputes US *elevator* for British *lift* to the desire to avoid suggestions of erections, surely he goes too far, the motive being more likely the American hankering after airs of importance by multiplying syllables for commonplace things, like *precipitation* for *rain,* or *gratuity* for *tip.* He wonders that Americans call a *buoy* a *boo-y* and implies that they do so to avoid the embarrassment of saying sometime, "Hey, look at that beautiful boy over there!" But actually, they pronounce the word with two syllables to avoid not sexual-social mortification but the ambiguity resulting from the use of the same sound for two strikingly different objects.

There's a whole section ("Language") in *The Amis Collection* devoted to dictionaries, as well as to usage, style, solecisms, and general corruptions in speech and writing. He applauds the practice in the supplemental volumes to the *Oxford English Dictionary* of now including sexual and excretory words shunned before, but he regrets the general pussyfooting with usage labels that might imply that people are of different kinds: "I wish [the editors] had more consistently faced the fact that they can do their duty as recorders of usage without abandoning their other duty of indicating what usages they, in common with other educated people, see as mistaken, ugly, harmful rather than helpful to the language." He means things like the misuse of *hopefully* for *it is to be hoped* and *scarify* meaning *to frighten thoroughly,* when it actually means *to wound* or *make an incision.* But he is not optimistic: it's possible that "about 1990" no one will know what is meant by such a usage label as *illiterate.*

Like other people of taste brought up on English literature, Amis is a severe critic of contemporary popular translations of the Bible as well as insensitivity to language in general religious practice. As he says, "No satirist would have dared to invent the real title of the (American) English translation of the Roman Catholic services: the New English Missalette." And what can one do but gag and then roll about on the floor confronted with the information that the new, improved rendering of

"Save me, O God, for the waters have come in
unto my soul"

is

". . . the waters have risen up to my neck!"?

"There is more in all this," he says, "than an appalling failure of
taste." There is the ruin of the only language available for Anglo-
Saxon religious experience. Making it clear that he is far from a
believer, Amis nevertheless asserts that religion must be understood if one is to participate in civilization. "A society in which it
was no longer possible to be a Christian would be as nasty as one in
which nobody could be a poet," and we are almost at that stage
already, what with no one's knowing very deeply or affectionately
the poetry of the past, not to mention the rudiments of meter and
form. The language of even journalism has decayed measurably
too: witness the rapid vulgarization of the London *Times,* carefully
proletarianized by Mr. Rupert Murdoch. Its style now is one "in
which it is impossible to discuss anything seriously."

Of course Amis is an avid collector of solecisms and malaprop-
isms, especially from elevated or pretentious sources. He recalls
hearing *perpetrate* for *perpetuate* not on the street but on the BBC
Third Program, and he remembers Prime Minister Edward Heath
publicly confusing *flaunt* with *flout.* He has practically given up
trying to remind people that *disinterested* does not mean *uninterested*
but refers rather to a now all-but obsolete attitude toward subjects
of study. He has lost heart to continue that particular campaign
because he has found that "those who don't notice what they say or
write don't notice what they read either." But he's not entirely
given up trying to stem the ruin of English punctuation, and here
something like an elegiac note creeps in. "When I was a lad, it was
illegal to hitch two sentences together with a comma: 'The dog
barked, I threw a bottle at him.'" But now Comma Fault goes

unrebuked everywhere, except in the stuffiest places, and Amis finds contemporary novelists the worst offenders. Again, no one seems to know how to use the hyphen any more, and we get *man eating tiger.* (Amis might have added that most people call a *hyphen* a *dash,* suggesting that they imagine them interchangeable, and well out of their reach anyway.) The apostrophe is also going out: too hard to learn, so away with it.

His copious collection of Wrong Words augments as time goes by: "Someone *alternatively* sulks in his tent and issues out to make statements, does not wish to *distract* from another's fine sporting performance, will not *detract* from any part of his planned speech and descends vigorously on all punctuation sins—however *venal.*" Similarly, a writer intending *derisive* writes *derisory,* one intending *credibility* writes *credulity,* and it appears that few writers hoping to make a splash can withstand the temptation to write *mitigate* when they mean *militate,* or vice versa. Amis's attentiveness has resulted in a virtual anthology of gaffes, of which this is a mere sample:

> We *unreservably* apologize.
> It is *inimicable* to the idea of a university.
> The food and surroundings were in *inexorable* taste.
> Americans really have a free press; it's
>   *incarcerated* in their Constitution.

There are, as usual, moral and social reasons for these embarrassments, usually "the hankering after an up-market synonym," the lust to come on grand, to show off as highly educated and impressive. But the real cause is more embarrassingly traceable to mass education, the current triumph of the visual over the auditory, and the general understanding that since all utterance is really a form of publicity or cover-up, it doesn't pay to take it too seriously. The fact is that "most of the men and women who use words in public don't care anymore which words they are, apart from a feeble hankering after the seemingly stylish. . . . How such people keep awake while they write is beyond me."

It is Amis's old-fashioned expectation that anyone who enjoys, indeed flaunts (*flouts?*) the identity of an author will have earned that right by an acquaintance with, if not a mastery of, a lot of the literature in at least his own language. Thus his shock and disgust one evening, playing charades at a party, to discover that playwright Arnold Wesker had no idea where "Oh, what a rogue and peasant slave am I!" came from. Play? Proverb? Book title? He didn't know, and Amis recalls, "among the spectators, I drew in my breath sharply." At that point, he says, he thought of "those writers, notably poets, who on the evidence of their writings, are not interested in the literary medium they use—no art, just 'statements.' Many of our cultural troubles start there." In Wesker's plays, "the air of being hastily translated from some other tongue is endemic to Mr. Wesker's dialogue." (E.g., "Ada suckles a beautiful baby.") This sort of thing, encountered repeatedly, we are to understand as one cause of Amis's loss of interest in the contemporary theater. He identifies himself as "a non-theatergoer who can read," and implies that the theater no longer attracts literary talent.

His view of things can't resist taking always a conscious verbal turn, as might be expected from a man who declares that in his dreams he constantly comes across reading-matter, "most often poetry of some kind." Instead of just saying that John Braine was naive and intellectually gauche, he writes, aware while writing of the words and the dictional-choice problem they pose, "Politically, John's behavior offered a choice of adjectives, among which 'naive' would be a popular choice, if perhaps an indulgent one."

As a novelist, he has said that he dislikes describing characters, preferring to let them describe themselves by what they say and by the idiom they choose to say it in. "The most powerful card in the hand of the novelist interested in character drawing" is "differentiation by mode of speech." *Lucky Jim* revealed very early that Amis is an extraordinarily sharp listener to spoken language, especially when used by those whose behavior he finds despicable. The awful Bertrand Welch's habit of clapping his lips shut after a final vowel in a domineering, pseudo-military, mock-aristocratic manner produces the significant *"You sam?"* and *"Got mam?"*, as well as, for hostelry, *"hostelram."* And acute attention to what people actually say, rather than what they are supposed to be saying, produces moments when characters not necessarily hateful but ordinary and careless lazily jettison consonants and say *mose people, corm beef, tim peaches,* and *foopball.* In *The Folks That Live on the Hill* there's this exchange:

> "I'm an old-fashioned pub landlord from way back
> . . . . We're on the way out. We're a dime breed."
> "Sorry, you're a what?"
> "A dime breed. Dine out like the dinosaurs."

(Amis says of Kipling, one of his strongest enthusiasms, "His diction was clear, with individual pronunciation of vowels.") As journalist Hilary Spurling has noticed, "dubious consonants and dodgy vowel sounds" are in Amis's fiction "an infallible sign of moral turpitude."

(Because Amis himself has said, "I try to make it a rule, when reviewing a book by a known friend, to slip in one adverse remark," I feel free to point out that in an essay of 1963, he allows *arguably* rather than *perhaps* to reach the printer, and in 1967 chooses the barbarous *basics* rather than *fundamentals* or *essentials.* But he was just a lad then and doubtless would be harder on himself now.)

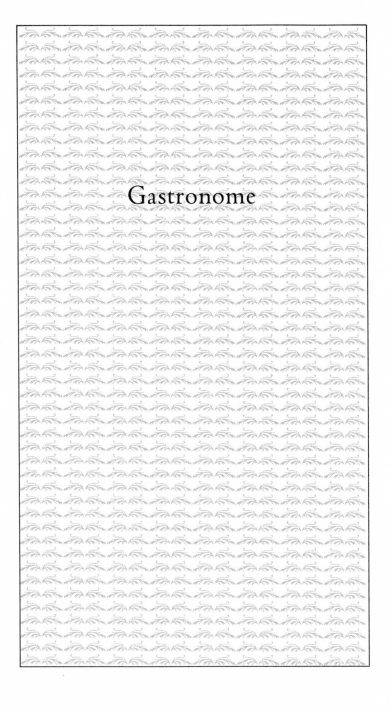

Gastronome

C RITICISM'' implies not so much carping or faultfinding as analysis, leading to assessment and valuation. Once you've learned, from experiencing literature or music or art, to criticize in the full sense, you can do it pretty well with anything. Like restaurants.

From September 1985 until January 1988 Amis reviewed restaurants monthly for the *Illustrated London News,* and from April, 1988, to August, 1993, for *Harper's and Queen.* Recognizing that restaurant criticism is like any other, more or less permanently interesting if decently written and focused on universals, he has included four sample performances in *The Amis Collection.* They make it clear that the same impulse animates his restaurant criticism as his other kinds: the quest for enjoyment, unmarred by anxiety about fashionableness and alert to the slightest hint of phoniness or fraud. His ideal restaurant would be managed by someone like Henry Fielding, said by Garnet Bowen, Amis's hero—and *alter ego* —in *I Like It Here,* to be

the only non-contemporary novelist who could be read with unaffected and whole-hearted interest, the only one who never had to be apologized for or excused on the grounds of changing taste. And how enviable to live in the world of his novels, where duty was plain, evil arose out of malevolence, and a starving wayfarer could be invited indoors without hesitation and without fear. Did that make it a simplified world? Perhaps, but that hardly mattered beside the existence of a moral seriousness that could

105

be made apparent without the aid of evangelical puffing and blowing.

"Reactionary"? Probably, but what does that matter where food and drink are the issue, where novelty is quite out of place, and where the hardest thing a restaurant manager must do is simplify and delete: cut out the music, canned or strolling; restrict cooking and preparation to the kitchen, avoiding showy salad construction and silly flames at the table; prevent waiters from reciting "specials"; repress the designer-chef's urge to make his products look like paintings (long ago Amis learned to "distrust any dish that appeals to the eye"); and eliminate the hype and fakery from the wine list and all needless French from the menu. All these are analogous to "moral seriousness" in writing and good workmanship there. Indeed, Amis notes, "It is tempting to say that a good restaurant, like a good novel or a good poem, is recognizable straight away, as soon as you cross the threshold." In his short story "Dear Illusion" he takes pains to associate a bad but critically celebrated poet with a bad but critically celebrated restaurant, closely resembling, actually, the once satisfactory Café Royal. It is the place chosen for a highly publicized ceremony honoring the bad poet Edward Arthur Potter, and Amis describes it as "a Regent Street restaurant famous until only a few years back for its food and service."

Crossing the threshold, what should the diner in search of excellence and value look for? Are pictures on display? "Restaurant art," says Amis, "gives you your social bearing." That is, the style of the pictures, their quality, tradition, and the assumptions behind their being displayed send fairly trustworthy signals about what you're going to get. Does the restaurant care enough about its "readers," as it were, to provide ample room between the tables? Is there good ventilation? General quiet, with a notable absence of music in any form? All important, for as Amis testifies, "I . . . have never had a decent meal in a disagreeable spot." A restaurant hoping for a good notice from Amis will provide a separate, comfortable, quiet place for drinks before the meal, and the bartender will be a master of the classic recipes. Arriving at the table, one should beware of the implications of oversized wine glasses: "I am all for vulgarity, but in its place, which is not in a serious restaurant." The quality of the bread and rolls is also to be seriously attended to, for "boring bread rolls" are "usually the sign of more boredom to come." Experienced clients of restaurants generally dislike prolix menus, but Amis is discriminating here as elsewhere. If the menu is well done, he doesn't object to some discursiveness: the menu at the White Tower restaurant he found "a most lively and informative document well worth a read-through."

He has given considerable thought to waiters as representative of national characteristics. The French, he has concluded, "are not really cut out to be waiters; the temporary but real power it gives encourages them to indulge their sense of superiority." Once, eating at Green's Restaurant, Amis was served by a waiter "who was evidently under notice":

> He imparted an international flavor, being very much the Frenchman in his obvious surprise, even disapproval, on hearing what I proposed to eat. British in bringing the wrong things and in not apologizing when this was pointed out, and French again in implying that differences at such a low level were pretty unimportant.

Italians and Greeks make the best waiters, Amis is convinced. They are friendly, with an instinctive suspicion of fraud, or at least an impulse to giggle in its presence. They would not be the best people to work at the currently stylish, costly London restaurant La Gavroche, gathering as if thrilled around the table behind each diner to whip off simultaneously the outsized pseudo-silver dish covers to reveal the awesome treasures beneath.

A good waiter in a good restaurant takes care that the bottle of wine shall be within reach of the diner and that he shall not appoint himself the agent of the diner's consumption or timing by secreting the bottle in such a way that his services seem continuously necessary. Because wines of some age and quality improve with a little airing, the wine list should be presented early—and what's wrong with having it on the table at the outset, like the salt and pepper? This will make it possible for "the chosen bottle [to be] delivered open before any food arrives." One affectation requiring instant rebuke by the conscientious critic is the wine-bottle basket in which a bottle of red is cradled as if an unspeakably precious artifact. These baskets impress bad people, and pretentious restaurants use them, sensing correctly that they are "the expectation of ignorant affluence." That is, well-to-do Americans, largely.

As must be clear by now, Amis's criteria as a literary and restaurant critic are strikingly similar, with emphasis on decent treatment of the customer and a suspicion of anything trendy or *nouvelle*. "Style" must not be allowed to override content, and the consumer is to be treated not as an inferior but an equal. Quoting a "food writer" saying, "A Hong Kong meal . . . is a statement to which customers are secondary," Amis says, "I know that sort of meal, and the statement is Fuck You, and you don't have to go to Hong Kong for it. Soho is far enough." The same motive that urges him sometimes to occupy a contrary position in literary criticism or to embrace a notably uncommon and unpopular view in general is visible here too, and not just in, for example, his refusal to be cowed by the snobbery attaching to French wines and his concomitant enthusiasm for vintages from Australia, Chile, Hungary, and other unfashionable places. For a snob wine writer to denigrate any wine triggers in Amis a compulsion to try it and, if at all possible, enjoy and praise it. Red sparkling Burgundy, for example, is considered vulgar by most elegant wine critics. As Amis says, "The American pontificator Frank Schoonmaker remarks that 'it is a wine regarded with amused contempt by most real wine lovers'." For Amis, that makes it "surely worth a try." And similarly, he has found that "Rosé wine is great stuff for flushing out the snobs."

Is it a commonplace among the sophisticated that hotel restaurants are usually disappointing? Then he will review a lot of them and delight in finding many admirable. They share at least one merit: because they are unstylish, there's little likelihood of encountering awful people there, notably "persons connected with the arts," especially "that section of them who like the dishes they eat to be adventurous, boldly innovative, exciting, etc." One of his reviews opens quite without shame, "When I go out for a meal I expect to enjoy myself at reasonable cost, not to learn anything or make any discoveries. . . ." Thus, a would-be favorable notice of Walton's restaurant in the *Tatler* delivers a valuable unwitting warning when it says that its cuisine "embodies a desire to create new, unusual combinations of flavors and textures." And any cuisine celebrated for its visuals is of course to be avoided, "failed designer food" being trendy at the moment. Once, dining at Boulestin, he reports that "the vegetable terrine put me off by being visually interesting." And at the Capital Hill restaurant, he found that "the salad had been designed not for eating but to look 'exciting' in a color-supplement photograph." But lest one think that he specializes in nasty comment because, for one thing, it can often be made funny, one should not overlook his pleasure in honest goods modestly presented—like his pleasure in, say, the novels of Elizabeth Taylor.

And he is less suspicious of novelty, as long as it's interesting and amusing, than one might expect. Trader Vic's, at the London Hilton, would seem precisely the sort of place unlikely to win approval, full as it is of bogus palm fronds, cute "tropical" drinks, and Americans. But far from satirizing it, Amis testifies that he had a wonderful time there, evidence of his willingness to be pleased so long as a place doesn't offend against his general critical criterion: could a well-disposed ordinary person enjoy it there and not be humiliated, not be swindled? But except at Trader Vic's and a few similar stunt restaurants, patronage by Americans generally has disastrous results. Their presumed demands for fanciness and elaborate shows of service have damaged the restaurant at the Ritz, and it is the American belief that "service" consists in the waiter's pouring your wine for you that has encouraged the staff to keep the bottle at an unreachable distance from the diner.

Curiously, as Hilly Kilmarnock says, it is precisely Amis's fondness for unfancy food—sausages and mashed potatoes, fish fingers, supermarket things like that—that makes him a fine restaurant critic. If the restaurant food isn't markedly better than fish fingers, why pretend? Amis is immediately identifiable when he enters a restaurant, unlike the inspectors for Michelin, who never identify themselves until after the meal, and not always then. Their trick is to pretend to be quite ordinary customers and see how they're treated. That's impossible for Amis, whose face and figure are too well known. Asked how he could do credible reviewing when the restaurant management can't help trying to give him exemplary food, drink, and service, he replies that when in these circumstances he's given a bad meal, he knows it's really bad. Considering his conspicuousness as a food critic, it's hard to believe the self-destructive rudeness and clumsiness he met once at Langan's Brasserie. There, he and his party, enjoying their preprandial drinks, were rushed importunately to their table so that, clearly, it could be rented again fast. The reward of Langan's was to find itself calumniated a month later in the *Illustrated London News,* whose audience is exactly the one Langan's hopes to attract. Ironic, for the food at Langan's proved to be excellent, and "writing and remembering has made me want to go again. But I won't."

He demands honesty and excellence particularly from restaurants thought of as "institutions." Like Rules, in Covent Garden, which presents itself as a guardian of the tradition of good, sound English cooking, in defiance of folklore emphasizing its stodginess. Amis's review is worth careful scrutiny. He begins by invoking, without apparent sarcasm, a series of totems of "England," the sort of things the restaurant likes to associate itself with in its publicity: George II, oysters, porter, Dickens, Thackeray, vintage port. The posted menu seems promising, with genuine English specialties: whitebait, potted shrimps, grouse, partridge, pheasant, mutton with caper sauce, eels. All prepared for a pleasant evening? Just wait.

The first let-down was the "rather cramped and overheated place" with only half enough seats for customers hoping for a cocktail in a quiet place before dinner. The drinks were fine and quickly served, but "the waiter tried to put me right on the orthodox recipe for the Old-Fashioned Cocktail." It soon became apparent that "some sort of quarrel was . . . going on among the staff," harmless, perhaps, although "in these matters slackness at the top is to be looked for."

"The move to the table brought a further lowering of morale." The banquette was too narrow, as if designed, on the USA fast-food-joint principle, to move the clients along quickly. But mean seating accommodation wasn't necessary here to perform that office: the food would have done the trick. In view of the terrible comments he's about to deliver, he is careful to note that "the wine was outstanding value and impeccably stored and served." Also, the coffee was fine. But except for the veal escalope and the whitebait, "everything else was"—not just bad, disappointing, or not up to the mark—everything else was *disgraceful*. The tomato salad was "woolly," the asparagus tasteless, some bacon "disastrously under-done." The venison was "as dry and void of flavor as anything I have ever tried to swallow." Even the simple English dish of sausage, onions, and mashed potato he finds he could have pre-pared better at home. The tripe was disgusting and the steak and kidney pudding dry and mean, with, as usual, "too little kidney, but of course only home cooks put in enough." All the entrees were served lukewarm on unwarmed plates, accompanied by un-dercooked vegetables. The two meals Amis ate at Rules prove memorable, but not in the usual sense: they were "two of the most disgusting full-dress meals I have ever tried to eat in my life." What a pity Rules associates itself with what is genuinely good and interesting in England and succeeds only in lowering yet further the reputation of English cooking. The cause is clearly, as so often, a moral one. Laziness, lack of supervision, lack of care, insufficient self-respect, cynicism, a general feeling that it doesn't matter. The same things that occasion bad writing.

Amis has abundantly earned the right to criticize by always himself giving more than expected, even where not much is expected. His little book *On Drink* is an example. It contains much more than the "Mean Sod's Guide" to cheating your guests of what they have a right to expect. The book is a learned, if informal, work about spirits, wines, and beers, with useful hints about glassware and techniques of mixing. But taken as a whole and read with care, it resolves into a treatise, sympathetic and funny, on human folly and the comic-pathetic predicament of being constrained and tormented by human impulses. That is, a substantial section is devoted to the physical—and metaphysical—effects of the hangover. Like all Amis's "minor" works, *On Drink* exhibits the same precision and thoughtfulness as his more deeply considered productions. Much facetiousness is present, but also much scholarship, and that word is appropriate. Almost everything Amis writes reveals what Karl Miller has observed, that "This is a writer who has done his stint of teaching English literature at university level." Even here. What other writer, what other "novelist" or "humorist," would recommend as a treatment for the metaphysical, that is, the guilt or "rue" hangover, a re-reading of *Paradise Lost,* XII, lines 606 to the end. These lines, dealing with the expulsion of Adam and Eve from Paradise, occur just after the Archangel Michael's final injunctions for the life to be led outside, now, of Eden. But all is not lost, for he tells Adam, if he will maintain Faith, and to it

> Add Virtue, Patience, Temperance, add Love,
> By name to come call'd Charity, the soul
> Of all the rest; then wilt thou not be loath
> To leave this Paradise, but shalt possess
> A paradise within thee, happier far.

But there's no time left for talk, and

> In either hand the hast'ning Angel caught
> Our ling'ring Parents, and to th'Eastern Gate
> Led them direct, and down the cliff as fast
> To the subjected Plain; then disappear'd.
> They looking back, all th'Eastern side beheld
> Of Paradise, so late thir happy seat, . . .
> Some natural tears they dropp'd but wip'd them soon;
> The World was all before them, where to choose
> Thir place of rest, and Providence thir guide:
> They hand in hand, with wand'ring steps and slow,
> Through *Eden* took thir solitary way.

In the midst of this passage, at lines 624–626, there's what Amis calls "probably the most poignant moment in all our literature." There, Eve expresses contrition for what she's done but finds comfort in knowing that it will be her offspring, ultimately, who will redeem mankind. Adam, who has earlier exhausted himself in scolding Eve, now hears her

> Well pleas'd, but answer'd not; for now too nigh
> Th'Archangel stood

to set in motion their banishment forever.

And Amis has emplaced, like an anti-personnel mine, this heart-rending scene, which is about the fears and hopes of all humanity, within a book which the jacket blurb designates "a witty, informative handbook for the drinker, both amateur and professional." Other suggested readings for the serious hangover sufferer are Solzenitsyn's *One Day in the Life of Ivan Denisovich*, which "will do you the important service of suggesting that there are plenty of people about who have a bloody sight more to put up with than you (or I) have or ever will have, and who put up with it, if not cheerfully, at any rate in no mood of self-pity." To raise morale in the gloomy hours of the severe hangover, battle poems can also be recommended, like Macaulay's "Horatius" and Chesterton's "Lepanto."

Saul Bellow is said to regard Amis as "an over-estimated writer affecting the high social style of club curmudgeon." Can that be the writer who dwells on the superb melancholy-hopeful ending of *Paradise Lost?* He is, thank God, much more complicated than that.

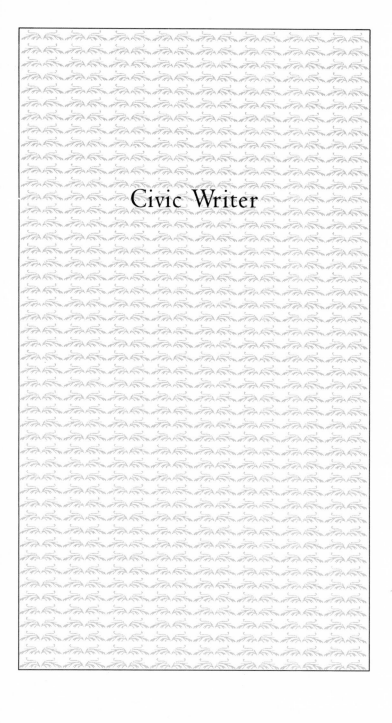

Civic Writer

O N E reason Amis is complicated is that it's hard to draw clear distinctions among his acts of criticism. Are they essentially literary, or social, or gustatory, or musical, or moral? They overlap maddeningly, as if everything bearing upon quality and its absence, and honesty and its absence, were his subject—everything except perhaps technology and science. A *civic writer* is what Karl Miller calls him: "He has spoken out with the utmost skill on a range of issues which have mattered to fellow citizens who have never read any of his novels." Norman Mailer used to look rather like that too, but with all the difference in the world.

The relation of low to high culture is a perennial Amis topic. It often boils down to the question, should an educated person watch on TV things like admittedly bad movies, vulgar game shows, and Hollywood sit-coms? His criticism of Richard Wollheim, author of a pamphlet *Socialism and Culture* (1961), is that although Wollheim discourses at length about mass culture, he seems not to have experienced much of it. "Mr. Wollheim approaches mass culture from the outside. . . . If he has ever watched 77 *Sunset Strip*, seen *Oklahoma!*, listened to a Connie Francis record, looked through a selection of keen neckties at a local outfitter's—and I mean as a *participant*, . . . not as one . . . in search of material about cultural trends . . . , he evidently feels this to be irrelevant to his task, even perhaps a bit shameful." If his understanding of popular culture were based on intimate experience instead of remote and sanitized observation, Wollheim would have a better understanding of "plural culture," the result of the contemporary blending of these formerly separated worlds. The merit of pop artifacts varies as greatly as the merit of elevated ones, and in popular culture, "the proportion of the really unreadable and unviewable and unhearable, though huge, is probably no greater than in the *whole* of high culture." Indeed, "the best of mass culture is very much better than the worst of high culture. Duke Ellington is not as good a composer as Mozart, but he is almost certainly more varied and adventurous than Leopold Mozart was." Besides, high and mass are not that distinct: each makes inroads into the other, so that in a piece of music, "we can have three and a half bars of popular culture, followed by seven of high culture, followed by five and a half of mass culture." (E.g., Gershwin, Bernstein.) If one attends to what's actually going on and can escape one's habitual artistic and generic snobbery, "it does almost look as if we shall have to judge all this stuff on its merits—just like literature and painting and that type of thing." What's needed is a clear-sighted and honest view of the cultural and entertainment and educational actualities. As Amis sees, and confesses, "Nearly all of us are implicated in mass culture, rather than confronted by it . . . ," and as he knows, bad Haydn is more repetitive and witless than good jazz.

Amis's literary-critical solicitude for the reader finds its corollary in his concern for other hapless victims, especially the victims of greedy, insensate, egotistical public and institutional mis-behavior. "Sod the Public: A Consumer's Guide" is what he calls an extensive (12-page) serio-comic, alphabetically arranged workout in *The Amis Collection*. It outlines techniques for screwing the public and making them like it, or at least concealing so subtly what's going on that the clients will mistake contempt and inattention for service and kind consideration. He begins briskly and without reservation:

"Sod the public" is the working slogan not only of government, the service industry and the retail trade, but also, as "sod the customer," "sod the audience" and other variants, that of interior designers, providers of culture, playwrights, composers, and many more.

Actors and actresses, being ignorant, lazy, and largely illiterate, constantly sod their audiences by mis-emphasizing lines, speaking them the way *they* want to speak them, to the ruination of sense and of the play. For example, Isabella's speech in *Measure for Measure:*

> O, it is excellent
> To have a giant's strength, but it is tyrannous
> To use it like a giant.

instead of stressing *use,* and making sense, an actress caring only about a cheap climax and "receiving attention and looking good," will stress *giant.* The public, sodded thus, "has nowhere else to go, except away, and is steadily being reduced to a state in which it listens only in a vague, general and inattentive spirit to the plays, films etc it pays to see."

Architects, especially the so-called post-modern kind, have a special privilege. "Most artists . . . have to get the public to watch or listen before they can sod it. . . . Architects are different. They have the unique power of sodding the consumer at a distance, not just if he lives or works in the building concerned, or just when he passes it a couple of times a day, but also when he happens to catch sight of it miles away on the skyline." One cause of all this sodding by artists is public subsidy, which pays "painters, writers and such *in advance.* This is a straight invitation to them to sod the public, whose ticket money they are no longer obliged to attract, and to seek the more immediate approval of their colleagues and friends." There's large irony here, for institutions like Endowments for the Arts and Arts Councils, which are supposed to encourage art and facilitate public access to it, turn out to damage real art and to repel the public from it.

Bookshops have found their own ways of sodding their customers. It's easier for them to re-stock if they categorize their paperbacks by publisher rather than by topic or type, and what does it matter if the searcher after a given author or title is sodded into wasting a lot of time? As long as the practice is easier on the seller, what does the convenience of the buyer matter? This is a low commercial form of the obsession that has damaged art and music and writing, best expressed by the shorthand term *club,* meaning, How will it go down at the club? That is, what will my fellow shopkeepers, wholesalers, publishers' representatives (cf. fellow artists, critics, etc.) think of it, and of me? So long as the in-group is impressed, sod the audience.

Dentists are now skilled in the game of sod the patient. The victim used to be allowed to sit, with some dignity, in a chair, but now he is forced to lie almost flat. "Nastier for you, producing feelings of helplessness among the old and nervous, but nicer for [the dentist] because he can sit down." This exemplifies the ideals of EFTA, or the Easier for Them Association, active everywhere in the developed world, but especially energetic, according to Amis, in Britain.

Pubs and bars are prime offenders, or were, until the public, tired of being sodded, fought back with CAMRA, the instructively successful Campaign for Real Ale, in contrast to what pubs preferred to purvey, the erzatz keg beer, easier to keep because jazzed up with irrelevant carbon dioxide, thus promising longer "shelf life." The EFTA principle the pubs had been observing before their defeat is echoed in the growing displacement of paper clips by staples. Easier for them to put in, harder for you to get out. Sod you. But probably the best illustration of the sod-the-public principle is the supermarket, now so familiar and accepted as to be virtually beyond examination or criticism. It makes you do the work, whereas before the grocer worked while you watched him. It's "a stunning example," says Amis, "of the sod-the-customer institution passed off as a public benefit." (Like something Amis, a non-car-owner, doesn't mention, "self-service" at gas stations. Why should the management hire an attendant when you can be sodded into doing his work for nothing?)

Travel and tourism provide abundant opportunities for sodding the public, and Amis's attention to both is a skirmish in his general campaign against stylishness and romanticism and slush and fakery. Travel in itself is all right. The trouble is that too often it results in travel books, and travel books are likely, or were in 1955, when Amis addressed this subject, to go in for Fine Writing of the more disgusting sort. They seem to prompt "an empty and indecent poeticism, apparently based on a desire to get into the next edition of *The Oxford Book of English Prose.*" It is Laurie Lee's travel book about Andalusia, *A Rose for Winter,* that occasions that stricture:

> The experienced reader will know what to do with a book whose blurb announces, as if in recommendation, its author's claim to "the enchanted eye . . . of a true poet." . . . One way of summing up this book would be to call it a string of failed poems —failed not-very-good poems too . . . .

that is, the sort crammed with bogus adjectives and meaningless similes. "Fragrant as water" is one Laurie Lee exhibitionistic locution, "which at first sight seems to mean almost nothing, and upon reflection and reconsideration is seen to mean almost nothing." Lee also offends by romanticizing, in the conventional literary way, the Spanish peasants, rhapsodizing over their "pure sources of feeling" and finding admirable their lack of learning and urban sophistication. All that's needed to explode these tired notions is a bit of literature: "Coleridge put Wordsworth right on peasants a long time ago."

A welcome counterweight to *A Rose for Winter* is Peter Mayne's *The Narrow Smile,* about the Pathan tribesmen living near the border between West Pakistan and Afghanistan. Mayne is welcome because he is not "the kind of travel-writer who feels obliged to demonstrate his sensitivity at every turn," but there's a romanticizing of primitive violence and some blurred moral discrimination even in Mayne's account of the Pathans. Amis observes: "Loyalty, genuine dignity, high spirits and independence are all valuable qualities, but they ought to shed their glamor when accompanied by arrogance, cruelty and bloodthirstiness; and the Pathan avenger with his rifle and knife is as contemptible, however much more impressive looking, as our own species of gangster with his razor or bicycle chain."

When Duckworth, the publishers, decided in 1974 to reissue Evelyn Waugh's delightful Mediterranean travel book *Labels,* they turned to Amis for an Introduction. He proved the perfect writer for this task, sharing most of Waugh's prejudices against fakery and the hype. He selects for special praise Waugh's classic moment of sentimental-travel-book satire, his treatment of Mount Etna at sunset:

> I do not think I shall ever forget the sight of Etna at Sunset; the mountain almost invisible in a blur of pastel grey, glowing on the top and then repeating its shape, as though reflected, in a wisp of grey smoke, with the whole horizon behind radiant with pink light, fading gently into a grey pastel sky. Nothing I have ever seen in Art or Nature was quite so revolting.

"It must have been a refreshment in 1930," Amis writes, "as it is now, to come across a travel book totally free of Mediterranean mystique, of any implication that the author is condescending to reveal some hint of his deep feeling for the ancient cradles of our culture." Amis delights in Waugh's exaggerated xenophobia and shares his willingness to exempt the Greeks from the general anathema, and it is a distinct relief for Amis to find someone not averse to dwelling on "the boredom and futility of sightseeing."

It is our loss that Amis has written no travel book. He has provided a sketch of one in "Amis Abroad," his 21-page account of a "Swan Tour" aboard the smallish Greek liner *Orpheus.* This took place in July, 1980, and I happened to be along too, together with my former wife, Kingsley's former wife Elizabeth Jane Howard, and the Powells, Anthony and Lady Violet. Amis's account of this tour, originally published in a cut version in the *Sunday Times,* is, as one would expect, very much in the de-romanticizing Waugh tradition, nor does he neglect the matter of "the boredom and futility of sightseeing." The *Orpheus* had just concluded a tour of the North British and Scottish coast and islands, and the problem faced by the Swan Tour people was how to get the vessel from Southampton back to Nice profitably, to begin from there a much more interesting tour of the Mediterranean. Thus this tour of numerous bits of religious and public architecture on the way, stopping at ports in France and Spain and Portugal and Spain again and France finally and using buses to transport the customers inland. The high intellectual and artistic quality of the tour, to distinguish it from just any old tourist operation, was guaranteed by the presence of a couple of learned art historians who did conscientiously describe and interpret the sights at a quite high level of intelligence and taste. How angry we all became in Barcelona, how demeaned we felt, to find the tour bus by some accident serviced by a guide-lecturer of the ordinary sort, a vulgar fellow who made horrible self-conscious jests as if we were not all of a finer weave than ordinary tourists. This tour was, as will be gathered, rich with opportunities for the student of snobbery, and Amis's notebook, although never conspicuous, was busy the whole time. I think he really enjoyed the two weeks, although it seemed clear that the idea of coming on this tour was his wife's, certainly not his.

On the tour were about two hundred people, oldsters, mostly (who else could afford it?), and the last four to join the ship at the Southampton dock, and just in time, too, were the Amises, who had somehow misread the instructions, and a bemused American couple who had thought 1300 hours meant three o'clock. The ship was hot and humid, and before long the service of lunch made it clear that there was to be no comfort from the cuisine. Everything was frozen (easier for them), and the food was "consistently unappetizing," including the bread made from equal parts of flour and preservative. The drinking scene was a little better: drinks were readily available, and some of the Greek wines were surprisingly potable.

The next morning—the *Orpheus* had arrived at Brest overnight—the Amises discovered what the two weeks were going to be like. Very early rising. Hasty, barely edible breakfast. Rush to the toilets for one's morning evacuation before the buses left. Then file into bus at quayside. Of course Amis immediately saw the military analogs of all this: reveille, usually in the dark; "in due course on parade with full equipment, namely (in my case) both pairs of glasses, passport, money, cheroots, lighter, pen, notebook, hat and Lomotil"—the last for stopping diarrhea in its tracks. The equivalent of military Orders for the Day was the program distributed the night before. Quasi-military also were the unexplained long delays and the necessity of enforced queuing up while being herded and controlled by guides very like NCOs of the more benign sort.

The first morning's touristic goal was a famous medieval stone-carved Calvary at Guimiliau church, which Amis found interesting, and he also discovered a shop which sold liquors, so he brought back bottles of rum and Scotch. The next port was Nantes, the shore-side event a tasting tour of a Muscadet vineyard and bottling plant. Although acid and undistinguished, the wine was served generously enough to occasion "giggles and little shrieks" when the group stumbled back to the bus. La Rochelle came next, where a bizarre sight greeted the group: along the perfectly ordinary, bourgeois sidewalk, a man came leading a tiger on a leash, clearly a show-off of the sort abominated by Amis. Rural churches well inland were that day's attraction, together with a superb lunch.

The following day was spent relaxing on the ship, crossing the Bay of Biscay to land at La Coruña, and about here Amis, despiser of "holidays," began to realize that he was enjoying himself. There was no lying-on-the-beach boredom but a structured fortnight with something to do and something, no matter how feeble, to engage the mind a bit. The alternation of work—sightseeing—

124

and doing nothing made this refreshingly different from the usual vacation, where you do nothing continuously. Santiago de Compostela was the first Spanish attraction, and Amis seems to have quite enjoyed this visit to the third shrine in Christendom, after Rome and Jerusalem. Lunch, very nasty now that France had been left behind, was served with appalling wines at the elegant Hostal de los Reyes Católicos across the square. The tourists had to be entertained during the afternoon while their ship sped to the next port, Vigo, where they would re-embark. Amis fled the "folklore" performance hoping to find something more interesting, but he ended wandering "fruitlessly around the torrid streets."

Next, Oporto, "dingy, dusty, rubbish-laden, . . . with its slums and political graffiti . . . ," the very antithesis of the magic towers and golden pavements of the romantic traveler's quest. Oporto kept Amis's critical talent from slumbering: the Moorish Hall in the Stock Exchange suggested nothing so much as "Paul Getty's card-room," and the Church of St. Francis was like "a provincial museum incompetently kept and seldom visited." It was a relief to look down into the Duoro Valley and behold at a distance the boats used to move barrels of Port along the river, boats with mouth-watering names on their sails like Sandeman and Croft.

The only thing Amis really enjoyed in Lisbon, what with the near-rotten seafood and the plethora of lame and blind persons, was the Gulbenkian Museum, which set off a rare burst of irrepressible enthusiasm: "I enjoyed it very much and advise anyone who gets within a hundred miles of it not to miss it on any account." Perhaps it's the contrast between this carefully organized, beautifully maintained oasis in the midst of so much misfortune and urban uninterestingness that grabbed him. One delight was a terracotta bust of Molière, by one J.-J. Callieri, who has made his subject "look like a good chap, and funny." Also admirable are a couple of Turners, a Fantin-Latour, and a Burne-Jones. No "modern" paintings at all, to Amis's relief and joy, because Gulbenkian bought what he liked, not what advisers told him he should like. For that, he becomes to Amis something like a minor saint of honesty and courage.

A brief stop at Portomão, and then on to sightseeing at Seville, where "the meal was of course filthy." This triggers an impulse to relate cuisine to national character, leading to "a straightforward inverse correlation between nations and their food-and-drink. Spanish, like English, nice people, nasty food; French, nasty people, nice food. Greeks, nice people, *terrifying* food." But there are difficulties with this paradigm, like "Italians, nice people, nice food. Danes too." But that exception can be equaled by "Germans, nasty people, nasty food." Better give it up.

Granada next. The Alhambra proved "a must for people who like climbing a lot of steps not very slowly in the sun with the humidity chasing a record." The day was concluded with a long, army-like wait in the dusty park of the Generalife. But if Granada was routine tedious stuff, Barcelona provided exciting outrages. First, the Picasso Museum, full of scratches and daubs testifying to that artist's lack of simple draftsmanly talent. "After Picasso we were taken, all unsuspecting in my case, to see that evidently major attraction of Barcelona, the Church of the Holy Family." Immune to publicity, Amis is always annoyed by artistic stunts and novelties, and he immediately locates in Gaudi's masterwork everything "self-aggrandizing and self-indulgent."

He had a quiet overnight to regain his good-nature while the ship made for Nice, "and suddenly, in a moment long foreseen but still suddenly, the cruise was over and a small brief sense of community gone. I had grown into the routine," and he admits he's going to miss it, hot, touristic, and sometimes boring and futile as it was. "Altogether, it was as pleasant a way of dealing with abroad—by not really leaving England—as I can imagine."

As that may indicate, what makes Amis's travel writing attractive is his half-comic, half-desperate timidity and vulnerability to the strange, which rapidly burgeons into the menacing. The understanding and portrayal of icy, paralyzing fear is one of Amis's

specialties not always sufficiently emphasized: one recalls poor
Charlie Norris in *The Old Devils*, terrified of being alone outdoors
in the dark. The moments of travel Amis seems to recall most
readily are less often the delightful ones than the horrors and
embarrassments. True, you can't be funny about the delightful
ones. Still—. Consider, in *I Like It Here*, Garnet Bowen's extraordinary anxiety about not being met as arranged at the port of
Lisbon. "Why isn't he here? Why isn't he here? Why isn't he
here?" Bowen asks "hysterically." "Darling, do calm down," says
his wife. Once his greeter shows up, Amis says of Bowen, "The
saturated solution of doubt, horror and despair that had filled his
veins was replaced in an instant by rich, oxygenated blood." The
disembarkation trauma was past, "but who could say what scars
were left upon the spirit by such prolonged, grave nastinesses?"
"Travel angst," he declares, is "a topic worth some study. I get it a
lot."

A particularly prolonged and grave nastiness occurred in France
in 1962. Amis dealt with it in a *Spectator* essay, "Something Does
Not Work with My Car." It is comic, but the anxiety is there, and
pressing. It begins as lateness anxiety. He's returning with his
family from Majorca in a rented car. Despite the tardiness of their
boat's arrival in Barcelona, there's still a good six hours to drive to
Narbonne, to meet the train which would carry them "almost to
Calais." Of course while Amis was sighing and tapping his foot on
the quay, all the other cars were ostentatiously unloaded from the
ship. His finally appeared. "We drove away . . . with just over
four and a half hours to go before train-time. Quite possible, with
a reliable car and no delays."

Those last phrases surely signal what's going to happen. There's
an hour-and-forty-minute delay at the French customs, and the
necessary acceptance of failure even causes some relief. "You can
relax now," he tells his wife, observing that no matter how fast
they drive, they're still going to miss the train. Soon, the clutch
gives out spectacularly, and they must push the car a considerable

way before finding a garage advertising repairs. This adds additional anxieties in the form of foreign-language trauma. After some linguistic frustration, the ruined clutch is inspected, and the garage owner informs Amis that they must stay overnight—in a hotel apparently owned either by the garage man or one of his relatives. Two days later the car was still not ready. The garageman, it turned out, could not find a replacement clutch and so "made one" himself. The Amises started off again and got 200 miles further towards Calais when, at three o'clock in the morning, the car stopped again. And again it required pushing. At seven that morning, Amis turned over the car to another garage, leaving it to them to return, if feasible, to the hire company. The Amises went on to Paris by train, and finally, after costly and humiliating hotel horrors, got back to England, sadder, wiser, much poorer, and badly shaken. Amis's travel writings thus hardly seem written with "the enchanted eye . . . of a true poet." They are something much better: reports of a critical and civic intelligence confronted with new objects to criticize. One might get the impression that Amis lacks zeal and enthusiasm, but he has those characteristics in abundance. They simply must be released by the right stimulus. Music, for example.

At Oxford, Amis and Larkin sustained themselves with New Orleans and Chicago jazz on the old three-minute, 78 RPM records, and both have written copiously and well on it. But Amis can't view jazz now without powerful elegiac feelings, for at about the time the Second World War arrived, jazz had died. Two causes did it in: it "began to lose its links with dancing and singing, the heart of all music"; and instead of being simply entertaining, it began to be studied in universities and "seriously" written about, in encyclopedias and jazz dictionaries. For Amis, the death of jazz and the loss of youth merge to become almost one subject:

> Jazz was the music that mattered, not only contemporary, happening all the time, but immediately attractive, no sooner heard than delightedly responded to. It was the music of youth, part of growing up, and as such, unofficial, unwelcome to authority, a piece of

underground culture long before the phrase was coined. It was Our music and They could only disapprove. . . .

But no more. Now young insolence must nourish itself on the tedious rhythms and banal repetitiveness and absence of elegance and mock-elegance of "modern" jazz, rock, rap, and such. Something invaluable has been lost forever, and it would be hard to say whether it's a style of music or one's youth.

But the civic writer is by definition more interested in the audience than himself, and the audience's likes and dislikes and the reasons for them must be a large part of his concern. A preview of the broadcast program of the Promenade Concerts for 1982 provides an opportunity to comment on various classical works and at the same time to dump on Modernism. Amis knows he has a lot of company here. He knows how many "hearts sink . . . at the phrase 'first performance'," and he has noted the rarity of subsequent performances of thousands, hundreds of thousands, of contemporary compositions designed to gratify the composers' friends and family but not the poor, long-suffering but still courteous audiences. "Twentieth-century music," he writes, "is like paedophilia. No matter how persuasively and persistently its champions urge their cause, it will never be accepted by the public at large, who will continue to regard it with incomprehension, outrage and repugnance."

In passing, Amis indicates the sort of music he does respect and relish: César Franck's "miraculous" Symphony in D Minor, Mozart's Piano Concerto No. 23, Brahms's First Symphony —where "the speed-up at the end of the last movement" suggests that Brahms (very like Amis, sometimes) was "bravely putting on a show of good spirits to hide his awareness that pain and sorrow do not go away." Another favorite is Beethoven's Piano Concerto No. 1, to which he has already paid homage in *Lucky Jim:* the rhythm of Beethoven's final movement lies behind the stresses in Jim Dixon's "Welch Tune," whose forceful if silent recitation provides one of Jim's few outlets for his hatred of Professor Welch:

You *i*gnorant clod, you *s*tupid old sod,
    you *h*avering, *sl*avering get . . .
You *w*ordy old *tu*rdy old scum, you *gri*ping
    old *pi*ping old bum . . . .

Beethoven's Eighth Symphony and Liszt's First Piano Concerto are also mighty acceptable, although the Liszt is an example of the deplorable and vulgar tendency (proto-modern, of course) to promote the soloist to a star role instead of leaving him or her an equal partner with the orchestra.

But for all his strong enthusiasms and dislikes, Amis knows his weaknesses as a writer about music and is happy to confess them. He plays no instrument and reads a score with difficulty. Choral music strikes him as woolly, and strings without other instruments, as in quartets, he finds "thin." His prejudices are right out in the open: he can't stand Mahler and most French composers and regards the choral theme in Beethoven's Ninth Symphony as "the most boring great theme in the world." And it's useless to rebuke him for these apparent insensitivities, he says, for he knows he's nothing but an amateur and "all amateurs must be philistines part of the time." But worse would be affectation or "to be coerced into showing respect when little or none is felt."

"My kind of music starts at about the beginning of the Eighteenth Century," with Bach, of course, but Bach's fault is excessive abstraction and indifference to the audience. Not so with Händel, a notably civic composer whose works are marked by "a superb masculinity." Then there are Vivaldi and Pergolesi and Telemann and C. P. E. Bach. And of course Mozart, offering in his music "a series of glimpses of a state of perfect order." And the best of Mozart is his piano concertos, especially, to Amis, K. 482.

If Mozart is for Amis "the greatest composer," Tchaikovsky is Amis's all-time favorite, partly because of his urge, again, very like Amis's own, to bury deep beneath a surface of unforgettable apparent levity, a solid stratum of passion and despair. Amis's comments on music sufficiently reveal his liability to intense emotion in the presence of inexplicable art. And just because his relation to music is amateur, he prefers music to literature. "I know enough about literature to be able to tell when a work takes a wrong or unfortunate turn," and he illustrates with Housman's "Fancy's Knell," where all's fine until something goes awry at the final four lines. Not so with music, where "I know just enough to know how much I miss." But, he continues, suggesting the way one might talk of religious experience if one could have it, "It is a great blessing to be able to catch glimpses of the world of mysterious, ideal beauty that music offers, even though I cannot truly enter it." I think he's not often spoken more seriously and emotionally than that.

Anthologist

PAYING attention to other people's music is an effective antidote for egotism and self-absorption. So is paying attention to other people's writing. Teaching literature is one way to do that. So is making anthologies. Amis has been an assiduous anthologist, and it's here that he has the opportunity to exercise scholarly values that used to be regarded by universities as their business, notably, intellectual curiosity and taste, as well as accuracy, textual reponsibility, and the conveyance of non-utilitarian knowledge.

Reviewing A. L. Rowse's *Quiller-Couch: A Portrait of "Q"* (1988), Amis praises Sir Arthur Quiller-Couch's perhaps surprising academic heterodoxy in reforming English studies at Cambridge, putting philology in its proper, subordinate place, and insisting that literature is "a living art, to be practiced as well as admired." But if Quiller-Couch's literary criticism—most of it originating as his academic lectures—is dead today, "where Q lives is in his anthologies," of ballads, Victorian poetry, and especially *The Oxford Book of English Verse* (1901; 2nd ed., 1939). Until in some ways superseded by Helen Gardner's *New Oxford Book of English Verse* (1972), this was the standard portable collection of English poems, and since it had few competitors (except Palgrave's *Golden Treasury of English Songs and Lyrics* (1861)) and could be found in almost every middle-class home, classroom, tutor's quarters, and editor's office, it had an incalculable influence on Edwardian and Georgian poetry. In the India Paper edition, it was the solace of countless

British soldiers in the trenches of Flanders and Picardy. Although Q had little ear for the contemporary, his taste for earlier excellence was secure. "I once spent a day," Amis testifies," reading all Michael Drayton's 150-odd sonnets, on the view that anything as marvellous as the celebrated 'Since there's no help' could not be the only good one. No; Q had picked the only winner." If taste was his forte, his fault was abridging and re-arranging and re-titling poems without notifying the reader. Making an anthology of his own, Amis caught him in several acts of editorial naughtiness. But such practices were not uncommon in Q's day, and he can be forgiven because of his rare virtues of learning and discrimination.

Amis devotes thirty-five pages of *The Amis Collection* to his reviews of thirteen anthologies, eleven of them collections of poetry. These commentaries offer him further occasions for lamenting the philistinism of cutting poems as well as for regretting the current general collapse of poetic talent, knowlege, and taste. What he finds most conspicuous in contemporary poems is "lack of finish, lack of art": "unrhymed poems must be swept quite clean of accidental rhymes and near-rhymes, and all poems must be gone over with a careful eye on similar word-endings: -tion, -ing, -y." And if free verse does promise a sort of freedom, it more certainly guarantees oblivion: "He who forgoes meter as well as rhyme forgoes memorability. . . ." Other favorite Amis themes given repeated airing here are the unfunniness of most "comic" verse, especially that committed by Americans, and the loathsomeness of most "nonsense" verse, the kind of thing the British at their worst specialize in and are actually proud of. Edward Lear is the best example, producer of unfunny limericks with their lazily repetitive final lines:

> There was an old person of Hove,
> Who frequented the depths of a grove;
>   Where he studied his books,
>   With the wrens and the rooks,
> That tranquil old person of Hove.

In reprehending that sort of thing, Amis instinctively adopts the position of "the reader," sodded again: Lear "deviates into sense and out of it again fast, constantly offering the reader the cup of reason and then dashing it from his lips."

Another topic Amis is fond of is the superiority of the war poetry of 1914–18 to that of 1939–45. Yes, Alun Lewis and Keith Douglas are OK, but not at all the equals of Wilfred Owen, Siegfried Sassoon, or Edmund Blunden. One reason is often overlooked: between the wars Modernism wreaked its damage on English poetry, as everywhere else. Another reason is less tendentious: the poetry of the Great War succeeds because of a "tension between style and subject matter," while "in 1939 there was none of that fruitful incongruity of style and material." That is, the means available to the later group of poets for registering irony had been coarsened and diminished largely to statement alone: a generally familiar "peacetime" style could no longer furnish by its echoes a tone of more subtle irony.

Amis's knowledgeable grasp of a literary "period" and its traditional interpretation is impressively registered in his review of Roger Lonsdale's *New Oxford Book of Eighteenth-Century Verse* (1984). This is an anthology powerfully influenced by the contemporary instinct for social justice and the recovery of respect to the lowly and inelegant. Unlike D. Nichol Smith in his earlier *Oxford Book of Eighteenth-Century Verse* (1926), Lonsdale has looked socially downward and located poems dealing with things not earlier regarded as acceptable eighteenth-century poetic subjects. Amis lists some of them: "The kitchen, prostitutes, a non-U wedding, golf, coalmines, street traders, builders, laudanum, homosexuality, a country fair, old soldiers, Whitbread's brewery, what it was like to be a woman, what it was like to be unemployed, what it was like to work on the land." And with an eye on such well-known eighteenth-century poets as Pope, Swift, Gay, and Gray ("the incumbents"), Amis notes that they wrote as if without knowledge of marriage and the family, or much interest in that subject, something that cannot be said of Lonsdale's poets. (One hitherto over-looked poem Amis singles out for praise is by one Captain H————, an address to his cold wife exhorting her to behave with more sexual passion ("Move, wriggle, heave, pant"). If Amis is hard on political-social trendiness elsewhere, here he is notably friendly to the new, more proletarian eighteenth century unearthed by contemporary scholars, many clearly motivated by dilute Marxist impulses of social fairness and folk egalitarianism. In addition, it is contemporary feminism in its academic dimension (thoroughly ridiculed in *Jake's Thing*) that has led to the recovery of the poems of Mary Leapor, whom Amis is happy to celebrate as one who "writes . . . with rare skill, reason and imagination on woman in society . . . in the general manner of Pope, with whom she has no need to fear comparison." All in all, "the book is a great catch."

As one thoroughly acquainted with the genre *anthology* and with the whole body of poetry in English, Amis is uniquely prepared to produce his own poetic anthologies, and so far he's made five of them. First, *The New Oxford Book of Light Verse* (1978) and in the same year, *The Faber Popular Reciter.* Then, in 1986, in collaboration with editor and publisher James Cochrane, *The Great British Songbook.* Next, in 1988, *The Amis Anthology.* And then, in 1990, *The Pleasure of Poetry.*

Anyone who thinks anthology-making is easy, that it is to be done in one's spare time or that it is so far down the "creative" scale as to resemble the art of compiling baseball or cricket records, might turn to Amis's lecture "Anthologies," "given"—an academic would say "delivered"—in 1980. There, he discloses that his research for *The New Oxford Book of Light Verse* took a whole year, and it's instructive to know also that Larkin, working on *The Oxford Book of Twentieth-Century English Verse* (1973) on a two-term leave from his duties as Librarian of the University of Hull, spent many lonely hours in the Bodleian Library, reading through its immense accumulation of hopeful thin volumes, in search of gems over-looked by more idle or careless predecessors. (He found remarkably few.) If one's name is on an anthology as editor one must admit no sub-standard work. Amis made this point forcibly in 1979 when

James Michie proposed that the two of them edit an anthology of short poems, none longer than thirteen lines as a way of excluding sonnets. Amis persuaded Oxford University Press to support the project and they began to work, despite Amis's and the publisher's doubts that there were enough good short poems to make a volume. Reading through "long afternoons at the London Library," Amis became convinced that the book would not be very good, for "a book of the size required could only be made by lowering the standard of merit in some proposed contributions to a lower level than I was prepared to accept." Amis consequently withdrew, Michie persevered, publishing the book with another co-editor, and the book did not do well.

Amis delighted in making both the *Light Verse* and the *Popular Reciter* because both required lots of reading, a luxury a novelist isn't always permitted to indulge in, writing every day being his self-imposed obligation. He began the *Light Verse* by deep consultation with his predecessors' collections, beginning with *Wits' Recreation* of 1641. After locating poets who seemed to have a knack for light verse, he went to their collected works to see how much they'd produced. There were many disappointments and much waste of time. "There was nothing to compare with coming across a single light poem by some monolith of sobriety, like Southey or Masefield, reading through his complete works in search of another, and finding just that one and no more." But sometimes the search was successful, turning up some nice Victorian titbits; a relatively unknown Victorian verse comic, Godfrey Turner; and John Byrom, already somewhat familiar but not as familiar as Amis's researches into his complete poetical works would make him. As a result of Amis's pleasure in Byrom and command of his work (he devotes six pages of the book to him), he can arrive at the original and probably correct view that Byrom's verse technique provided hints for Lord Byron's *Beppo,* and Byron was "the greatest writer of light verse we have ever seen."

While reading for the anthology, Amis was aware of three pressures: honoring his own taste, honoring "the tradition," and being conscious of his immediate "illustrious predecessor's" work, Auden's *Oxford Book of Light Verse* (1938). "Reconciling these three pressures," he says, "made the task of preparing a text quite good fun in its way." When he had finished collecting his poems, he found he had twice as many as he needed, and reducing the number drastically required a further consideration: familiarity. "The best light poems had been anthologized many times before. Should that be a deterrent?" Here he invokes Quiller-Couch, who laid it down that "the best remains the best even though a hundred judges have declared it so." (Amis has never forgotten hearing an Oxford don tell what he'd learned by being at Oxford: he said, "Don't be afraid of the obvious.") Yet, says Amis, "an editor feels he must add something," so for some entirely new things he went to his friends. Anthony Powell contributed a masterly Dryden-esque satire on the Scots, "Caledonia," which should be better known: the Scots are

> a Race, whose Thought and Word and Deed
> Have made a new INFERNO *North of Tweed,*
> Where they can practice in that chilly HELL
> Vices that sicken; Virtues that repel.
> * * *
>
> What are this Race whose Pride so rudely burgeons?
> Second-rate *Engineers* and obscure *Surgeons,* . . .
> Such Mediocrity was ne'er on view,
> Bolster'd by tireless *Scottish Ballyhoo*—
> Nay! in two qualities they stand supreme;
> Their *Self-advertisement* and *Self-esteem.*
>
> What of this Land of which they love to talk?
> The Sons of SHEM ascend its hills to *stalk,*
> And men with nasal *Twang* in *Harris Tweed*
> From THE AMERICAS to these succeed.
> More rich than CROESUS they have cross'd the Main,
> To slay the *Grouse* and quaff the dry *Champagne.*
> They seek for *Salmon* in *the bonny Brae,*

While *Wall Street* Banks their *bonny* incomes pay;
But Orange-Peel and Cigarette-end ride
On the dank waters of the slimy Clyde
And careful Scots, against a rainy Day
Wade in and bear these Treasures all away.

And Robert Conquest helped out by contributing a number of his hitherto private limericks. For example,

A young engine-driver called Hunt
Once took out his engine to shunt,
   Saw a runaway truck,
   And by shouting out, 'Duck!'
Saved the life of the fellow in front.

Working on his own *Light Verse* and necessarily attentive to Auden's editorial choices and practices, Amis found himself in profound and significant disagreement with Auden's concept of "light verse." Auden's idea of light verse reflects the convictions of a socially and politically sentimental fellow-traveler of the 1930s. Thus for him light verse embraces folk-songs, poems about everyday life, and nonsense poetry. To Auden, what's necessary for the flowering of these things is commonality and community, where the poet feels not a part of a separate "leisured class" but at one with the masses. ("Solidarity" is the key word.) In the nineteenth century, alas, there arose a social class "who had independent incomes from dividends," which tended to alienate them from the people. "As the old social community broke up," Auden writes, "artists were driven to the examination of their own feelings and to the company of other artists. They became introspective, obscure, and highbrow." For Auden, thus, light verse is an emanation of the folk, or from those convinced of their "solidarity" with it. For Auden, Burns becomes a hero of light verse, not because he's funny but because his poems seem at home among the folk. At the end of his Introduction, Auden abandons completely his announced obligation to define light verse and hurls himself into hasty pseudo-socialist observations about "the modern poet" and "society," the sort of thing almost obligatory in his day. "The problem for the modern poet," he says, "as for everyone else to-day, is how to find or form a genuine community in which each has his valued place and can feel at home."

All this is, to Amis, close to absolute nonsense. For him, light verse arises not from the folk but from the learned, and specifically from their deep familiarity with high poetry and their natural human impulse to parody it or to deflate its occasional pomposities. In short, light verse is gravely insincere and usually subversive of good order, high-mindedness, and "community." In England it probably began as a reaction among the witty and skeptical to the Frenchified style of Restoration poets with their highfalutin' neo-classic odes, elegies, and pastorals. Far from being about "life," as Auden would have it, light verse is about literature. A good example is the Victorian Lyman Blanchard's "Ode to the Human Heart," which of course Amis prints and Auden does not. Here, each of the eight four-line stanzas consists of nothing but the most hackneyed lines of English poetry, newly arranged with a satirist's regard for a kind of "sense":

> Music hath charms to soothe the savage breast,
>> Look on her face, and you'll forget them all.
> Some mute inglorious Milton here may rest,
>> A hero perish, or a sparrow fall.

or,

> My way of life is fall'n into the sere;
>> I stood in Venice on the Bridge of Sighs,
> Like a rich jewel in an Ethiop's ear,
>> Who sees through all things with his half-shut eyes.

Proceeding in the opposite direction, Auden's obsessions with popular and low life impelled him to include Kipling's "Danny

Deever," surely one of the unfunniest, unlightest of poems, indeed, "one of the most harrowing," as Amis says, "in the language." From Auden's point of view, any poet's focus on folk-life or simplicity qualifies him as a light-versifier. Thus he includes Chaucer's "Miller's Tale" and "Wife of Bath's Prologue," as well as "Adam lay ibowndyn," a sincere and moving celebration of what theologians once called the Fortunate Fall. Paradoxical, yes, but not funny at all. Assuming somehow that angry satire is "light verse," he includes Siegfried Sassoon's "The General," whose ending is more likely to occasion tears than smiles:

> "Good-morning; good-morning!" the General said
> When we met him last week on our way to the line.
> Now the soldiers he smiled at are most of 'em dead,
> And we're cursing his staff for incompetent swine.
> "He's a cheery old card," grunted Harry to Jack
> As they slogged up to Arras with rifle and pack.
>   * * *
> But he did for them both by his plan of attack.

Auden also includes blues lyrics, despite, as Amis notes, "Their recurrent themes of betrayal and murder."

Amis's vigorous dissent from Auden's definitions illuminates the distance between the "socially conscious" observer of the 1930s and the infinitely less-illusioned editor of the 1970s, instructed by the exposure of a lot of community-living stuff and other progressivist rhetoric as vaporous cant, and instructed also by the Second World War, with such outcrops of community action as the Katyn Massacre. As Amis notes, "Auden's political preoccupations . . . led him . . . to foresee a planned egalitarian state of society in which light verse would flourish as never before." He was wrong on both counts, and despite Amis's admiration for Auden's poems—those, that is, dating from before his decamping to the US early in 1939, to avoid, as many thought, participating in the forthcoming war—he has little respect for Auden's political and social sense. Reacting against Auden's views about poetry and society, he's quite content to have his own book known as a reactionary anthology. When Larkin published his *Oxford Book of Twentieth-Century Verse* five years earlier, he conceived it an exemplary registration of his own anti-Modernist taste—hostile to free verse, for example. He liked to think that Amis, in editing *The New Oxford Book of Light Verse*, would be conducting a similar anti-Modernist campaign. He wrote Amis, "We shall have stamped our taste on the age between us in the end."

Since the bulk of Amis's light-verse selections come from well before the age of Modernism and they are funny, attractive, and even memorizable, the book becomes an exhibition of the efficacy of meter and rhyme in preserving useful observations delightfully. There are a few poems from the eighteenth century—Swift, Gay, Byrom—but distinguished light verse clearly belongs to the nineteenth century, when a strong current of popular high poetry established a back-drop for its wry, comic refraction in the hands of such Victorian masters as W. M. Praed, C. S. Calverley, W. S. Gilbert, and J. K. Stephen. One thing clear is that light verse in the Amis sense can arise only when politics assumes sophisticated bourgeois verbal forms: it thus belongs to a limited, non-reproducible moment, well before the twentieth-century age of political hysteria, overstatement, and violence. Somehow, light verse belongs to an age when it was possible to assume that politics doesn't matter, or inevitably assumes comic forms. That age is long past, and so is the age of light verse.

Although he is kind enough not to say so, Amis can have little admiration for Auden's editorial laziness. In fact, one way to value Amis's work as an anthologist is simply to compare his understanding of editorial responsibility with Auden's fecklessness. Auden finished his *Light Verse* just before leaving on his trip to China with Christopher Isherwood, and he allowed Mrs. A. E. Dodds, wife of Oxford professor E. R. Dodds, to finish up the scholarly chores like checking the texts and the notes and doing the proofreading. (Auden dedicated the book to Professor Dodds, thus ignoring the convention that an editor does not "dedicate" an anthology, most of it constituting the work of other authors, usually his superiors.) Anxious to get away, Auden wrote the Introduction rapidly. Mrs. Dodds told the publisher: "All Mr. Auden's typescripts need checking. He gave me the references from memory and a good many are wrong. Also some poems are taken from inaccurate versions." Finally, she and an editor at the press had to finish the book themselves, sometimes actually selecting the poems.

An example of Auden's way with texts is his dealing with the eight-stanza comic-obscene "Hye Nonny Nonny Noe," originally found in John Aubrey's seventeenth-century *Brief Lives.* The meaning hinges entirely on the absence of a comma at the end of the penultimate line of each stanza. Inserting a comma, as Auden (or Mrs. Dodds?) does, changes the last lines from wonderfully saucy substantives to mere tedious refrains. Here, for example, is the third stanza:

> Sweet she was, as kind a love
>   as ever fettered swain;
> Never such a dainty one
>   shall man enjoy again.
> Set a thousand on a row
>   I forbid that any show
> Ever the like of her
>   hye nonny nonny noe.

And even more striking is the end of the next stanza:

> Hair she had as black as crow
>   from the head unto the toe
> Down down all over her
>   hye nonny nonny noe.

How, with his instinct for the naughty, could Auden have missed the point? But miss it he did, and furthermore he prints without explanation only three of the eight stanzas and supplies a bogus title, "She Smiled Like a Holiday," using (and misquoting) a line from well inside the poem.

Against Auden's Introduction, a superficial light essay, one can place Amis's, almost twice as long, a solid, learned, critically powerful and historically informed inquiry into the subject. Here, Amis makes the point emphatically that light verse requires a simultaneous tradition of serious verse familiar to the reader. It operates by using all the formal techniques of high poetry but applies them to trivial things. And as Amis says, "High verse could exist without light verse, . . . but light verse is unimaginable in the absence of high verse." And the high verse here is largely that produced by the poets of Amis's B. Litt. thesis. Far from emerging from the folk and addressing them, light verse "is altogether literary, artificial, and impure." And it must be technically perfect, even more perfect than the high verse it apes. It requires "careful finish," and the best examples exhibit "the effective surmounting of self-imposed technical obstacles."

Is nonsense verse, like Edward Lear's, properly considered light verse? Not really, and Amis despises it because of its distance from genuine wit, an activity of the sophisticated, not the childish, mind. Indeed, he goes so far as to assert that the British fondness for nonsense verse constitutes a distinct blot on the national character, betraying its self-satisfied fondness for "the arch, the twee, the whimsical, etc." It is a tendency that "disfigures English literature, humor, even character." Lear's "The Pobble Who Had No Toes" (sample line: "He tinkledy-binkledy-winkled a bell") marks "one of the great nadirs of our national intellect and feeling." Lear's shoddy limericks are evidence of "the damaging blot on our culture: amateurishness, the notion that a gentleman . . . never need do anything properly and that only drudges and artisans see the job through." (Examples: Auden's conduct of his *Light Verse;* and British publishers' habit of presenting bibliographies any old way, with the works arranged neither chronologically nor alphabetically. Sod the public, literary department.) Nonsense poetry lacks the gently subversive quality of genuine light verse, although both might seem to perform light verse's function of raising "a good-natured smile."

Amis concludes his essay by observing how very little light verse is around today for the anthologist to collect. The reason is simple and obvious, as well as disheartening: "Light verse has declined because non-light verse has collapsed." Contemporary poetry without notable form cannot provide a background for light verse, for which form—both metrical and stanzaic—is essential. His examples of contemporary light verse are thus few and spotty. There's Betjeman and Larkin and Amis himself, D. J. Enright and Gavin Ewart, but desperation conducts him finally to George MacBeth's "The Political Orlando," where the ironic statement supplies everything and the technique (free verse) nothing. It's clear that to have real light verse you have to have a general audience for "poetry," and currently there is none.

That there once was a large, enthusiastic, and powerful one is the point implied by Amis's next anthology, *The Faber Popular Reciter*. If, as he says, the *Light Verse* anthology took a year to make, "ninety-five percent of the contents of the *Reciter* was in my note-book after a couple of evenings with *The Oxford Dictionary of Quotations*." He found that the kind of rousing popular verse he was collecting stopped being produced about 1914, and surely by 1918, when it became difficult or embarrassing to advertise "confidence in your civilization and its values." And indeed the most recent poets Amis has found to represent the tradition he's celebrating in the *Reciter* are John McCrae, Rupert Brooke, Alan Seeger, and Julian Grenfell, authors of soldier poems written in the days before the Great War became something that seemed to invite only ironic treatment. To realize what Amis is saying, imagine someone today writing a stirring, non-ironic, wholly patriotic and unforgettable narrative poem, like Macaulay's "The Armada," celebrating the Normandy landings in June 1944. What has happened to us? Why can't we memorialize in poetry the bravery—there's no other word for it—of the soldiers on Omaha

Beach who one after the other extended the bangalore torpedos under the German wire as one after the other they were shot and blown apart, until finally one succeeded? Why can't their behavior be celebrated in the sort of poem that persuaded nineteenth-century readers that some values, at least, were admirable and secure? In the right hands, such a poem could be written without any recourse to discredited diction like *gallantry*, and such a poem might reconcile readers with poets once again.

As so often in Amis, there's an undeniable elegiac tone in his Introduction to the *Popular Reciter.* This kind of public poetry fit for recitation was, a century ago, virtually synonymous with "poetry." But "that, together with much else, has gone." A few echoes do reverberate. As late as 1948, according to James Kirkup, a woman named Elsie performed poetry recitations at Speakers Corner, Hyde Park, specializing in selections from *The Rubaiyat,* Burns, Kipling, Masefield, and Newbolt. Henley's "Invictus" was a favorite, and so was Shelley's "Ozymandias." All are included in Amis's anthology, together with numerous military, naval, and patriotic pieces, fruits of life before the age of conscription, draft-dodging, coercion, and military chickenshit. (With Sassoon's "The General," compare Prince Hoare's "The Arethusa": "A health to our captain and officers true.") Macaulay's "Horatius" is in and so are Newbolt's "Vitaï Lampada" and similar celebrations of heroism. Popular religious comfort was still a theme for poems turned hymns, like "Abide with Me" (popular with the aging and aged, and certainly an Amis favorite: he includes it in all three of his "serious" anthologies). Some of the popular poems are popular because they encourage self-respect, like Landor's "I Strove with None" and Dryden's "Happy the Man." Other popular themes are magnanimous behavior, the yearning for rural retirement after the noise and corruption of the busy world, and the ubiquity of death and its ultimate desirability. The poems Amis has chosen to convey these themes are to him exemplary, for they are "neither egotistical nor formless," and they tend to produce a communal effect, emphasizing "what unites the individual with some large group of his neighbors"—unlike many Modernist poems, whose effect is to separate the poet and his clever reader from the dolts and philistines who make up the rest of society. Technically, these poems are distinguished by "clarity, heavy rhythms, strong rhymes": these are "the vehicles of confidence, of a kind of innocence, of shared faiths and other long-extinct states of mind." Drayton's "Agincourt" is a good example from long ago, and more recent specimens Amis exhibits are Thomas Campbell's "Ye Mariners of England," Browning's "Incident of the French Camp," and A. C. Benson's "Land of Hope and Glory." Even the Americans in patriotic mood are called upon, and we have "The Star-Spangled Banner," Emerson's "Concord Hymn," Julia Ward Howe's "Battle Hymn of the Republic," and Lowell's "Once to Every Man and Nation," not to mention lots of Longfellow and Whittier. There's something about the combination of innocence and nobility in Amis's selections that makes it hard to read through the anthology dry-eyed, causing one to notice, again, how few modern poems produce this humbling and salutary effect.

And perhaps this is the place to notice the way an anthology reveals its maker almost as forcefully as a written confession or testimony. Unlike an author like Sylvia Plath, an objective writer like Amis tends to refract his emotion and significant moments of his secret life by treasuring and recommending works by others. He seems to be suggesting the kinship of his own poems and those of others he anthologizes in the way he presents the list of books "Also by Kingsley Amis" opposite the title-pages of both *Memoirs* and *The Amis Collection.* Except for the collaborations, he arranges his books in three categories: fiction, verse, and non-fiction. There is no category for "anthologies" or "editor." Under *verse,* he lists not just *A Case of Samples, A Look Round the Estate,* and *Collected Poems,* but his anthologies, with "editor" acknowledged for each. He clearly is in no way ashamed of works which involve literary-creative activity in some ways parallel with his original poems.

The communal as opposed to the egotistical receives a further celebration in Amis and Cochrane's *The Great British Songbook.* People like to sing together, Amis observes in his Introduction, but although they remember the melodies, after the first few lines of a song they've forgotten the words and have to descend to humming or silence. "So what we are doing in this book," he says, "is providing the words everybody has forgotten for the tunes everybody remembers." An essential criterion for inclusion is that "every song must be a *song,*" associated with a definite tune, which cuts out literary lyrics like "Crossing the Bar." An elegiac and anti-Modernist note is of course struck here too: "One cannot help noticing that the last acknowledged British poets to produce words that could be turned into memorable songs were Housman, Newbolt, Kipling, and Masefield." Amis's Introduction and explanatory remarks in the text reveal how deeply and continuously he's attended to the popular mind, especially its distance from the adversarial stream of high culture. All he writes, and all he collects, introduces, and annotates, implies his regret at what the modern world has done to itself by encouraging solipsism, egotism, and the pride of class- and race-divisiveness. Clearly we are in the presence of someone who is not a mere popular novelist. Here is a writer who lives in history, and not just political history but social, cultural, artistic, and theological history as well. That is why his "non-fiction" sometimes seems more essentially "Amis" than his novels.

Of all his anthologies, and almost all his books, including *Memoirs,* the most autobiographical is probably *The Amis Anthology,* whose publisher purveyed it as "A Personal Choice of English Verse," an emphasis Amis sanctioned in his Introduction, where he said, "This is a collection of my favorite poems, which is not the same thing as a collection of the couple of hundred English poems I happen to think are the best. A favorite poem, like a favorite human being, is attractive partly for reasons that are the stronger for being unfathomable. There has to be a personal element about such a poem, something producing the illusion that it was written specially for me. . . ." And if we are to judge by the tenor of these "favorite poems," the person who made *The Amis Anthology* is one forced by essential melancholy and despair to put on the masquerade of wit and gaiety. The poems as if "written specially for me" convey a pervading sense of loss and emptiness, a deep consciousness of the pathos of mutability and evanescence. Despite occasional moments of levity, most of these poems release the emotions appropriate to death and grief. What he says of Betjeman his anthology says of himself: "He is always taking us from the reassuringly familiar, sometimes bland, surface of things to the unpleasant underlying facts of death, loss, pain, illness, grief." The reasons Amis treasures these poems so personally are far from unfathomable: they are perfectly clear, and they speak of a sensitivity to sorrow and pain that might be unendurable except for the ironic wit and critical skepticism that war against it.

The pathos of time is the burden of the very first poem Amis has selected, by the fifteenth-century John Lydgate. The poem is "Lyarde," about a superannuated horse put out to pasture. He resembles his human betters, once energetic, able, and resourceful, but now inevitably on the shelf:

> Whosos cannot do his deed, he shall to park,
> Barefoot withouten shoon, and go with Lyarde.

If a reader begins with this poem and goes straight through the book he will come upon repeated adversions to the theme of loss and evanescence:

> My youth is spent . . . .
> Chidiock Tichborne

> Like to the falling of a star, . . .
> Even such is Man, whose borrowed light
> Is straight called in, and paid to night.
> Henry King

Sweet rose . . . ,
Thy root is ever in its grave,
And thou must die.

George Herbert

. . . at my back I always hear
Time's winged chariot hurrying near.

Andrew Marvell

Poets themselves must fall, like those they sung;
Deaf the praised ear, and mute the tuneful tongue.

Alexander Pope

No renewed hostilities invade
The oblivious grave's inviolable shade.

Samuel Johnson

. . . all that beauty, all that wealth e'er gave,
Awaits alike the inevitable hour.

Thomas Gray

. . . those blest days when life was new,
And hope was false . . .

Thomas Love Peacock

And selecting from Keats, it is of course the "Ode on Melancholy"
Amis chooses, for melancholy

dwells with Beauty—Beauty that must die.

Selecting from Tennyson, he turns from "Ulysses," with its
celebration of strenuous life, and chooses "Tithonus," where everything is caught up in mortality except the lone, eternally un-
happy speaker:

152

The woods decay, the woods decay and fall,
The vapors weep their burden to the ground,
Man comes and tills the field and lies beneath,
And after many a summer dies the swan.
Me only cruel immortality
Consumes . . . .

There's Stevenson's "Requiem:

Under the wide and starry sky,
Dig the grave and let me lie,

and Housman's "Bredon Hill":

When the snows at Christmas
    On Bredon top were strown,
My love rose up so early
    And stole out unbeknown
    And went to church alone.

In Housman's "Fancy's Knell" there's the flute-player's awareness
of the equal brevity of the music and the musician:

To-morrow, more's the pity,
    Away we both must hie,
To air the ditty
    And to earth I.

(It's perhaps the directness, almost the literalness, of these final
lines of the poem that Amis elsewhere found inconsistent with the
tone of the preceding lines.) Housman concludes "The Lent Lily"
by emphasizing that the daffodil, whose brief life-span has fasci-
nated English poetry from the outset, like the Lenten lily "dies on
Easter day." A reason for Amis's fondness for Housman lies in his
observation that Housman was a master of "the old primary

themes of loss, pain, and deprivation." In Henry Newbolt's "The Nightjar" the beautiful injured bird dies, and

> O how I wish I might never forget that bird—
> Never!
>   But even now, like all beauty of earth,
> She is fading from me into the dusk of Time.

As it rains, Edward Thomas is to be found "remembering again that I shall die." ("Haunted by the sense of mortality" was Thomas, as Vernon Scannnell has observed. That sense is a virtual ticket of admission to *The Amis Anthology*.) Even in the scanty poetical works of T. E. Hulme, Amis finds what he's looking for in this complete little Imagist poem:

> Old houses were scaffolding once
>   And workmen whistling.

Modernism, it proves, can't do much poetically with the topic of death, and the kind of poem Amis relishes tends to disappear about the middle of the twentieth century, although Auden has moments when he adverts to the earlier traditional obesssion with time and change:

> Time watches from the shadow
>   And coughs when you would kiss.

And Amis does not overlook Larkin's "Cut Grass":

> Cut grass lies frail:
> Brief is the breath
> Mown stalks exhale.
> Long, long the death
>
> It dies . . .

But that's about as modern as Amis goes. There's no D. H. Lawrence in his personal collection, no Wallace Stevens, and of course no Samuel Beckett or John Ashbery. No Pound, naturally, and no Eliot, although it's curious that he's not been seized by Eliot's "New Hampshire," which would seem perfect for his emotional purposes, with its

> Twenty years and the spring is over;
> Today grieves, to-morrow grieves,
> Cover me over, light-in-leaves. . . .

If one revealing autobiographical feature of *The Amis Anthology* is the funerary or elegiac tendency of many of the poems, another is the learned enthusiasm and pedagogic gusto of the explanatory notes. It is here that he courteously but firmly exposes Auden's insensitivity to the meaning of the phrase *Hye nonny nonny noe,* and it is here that he quietly sets right Margaret Drabble, editor of *The Oxford Companion to English Literature,* who has there confused Reginald Heber's dates with his half-brother's. But there's a lot more in these thirty-four pages of notes than the correction of error.

As he says in his "Note on the Notes," "Some of these notes provide information. They are meant to explain difficult words and what may be obscure references, in the belief that the better a poem is understood, the more interesting and enjoyable it becomes. . . ." And some notes "bring in matters of personal reminiscence and reaction that may not be out of place in an anthology such as this." Thus, for example, his note on George Peele's "Song: Whenas the Rye Reach to the Chin," which quotes "my true love" saying that until spring comes round again, "She could not live a maid." "This song," Amis says, "surprised the young Amis by showing that proper poetry could be about *that* too." These notes reveal that Amis commands English literature more impressively than most professors of English. In glossing a seventeenth-century appearance of *chameleon,* he offers the information that "it was generally believed that chameleons fed on air. Hamlet thought so, or so he said." Only occasionally do the resources of the London Library let him down. Of Samuel Johnson's "Prologue to *A Word to the Wise,*" he confesses that he can't discover the author of the play, whereas a more thorough academic search would have revealed the author to be the Irishman Hugh Kelly, whose comedies were popular in London in the late 1760s and early 1770s. Amis's extraordinarily careful reading of poems most readers treat superficially—as "examples" of this or that general tendency—is evident in his comment on Thomas Gray's "Ode on the Spring." Observing this poem's surprising turn away from the conventional which it has led a reader to expect, "This is exactly the poem," Amis says, "that might have been written by a clever fellow who had heard the 'Elegy Written in a Country Churchyard' praised just once too often." And in dealing with the "Elegy," he devotes a page and a half to a full-dress inquiry, virtually a brief scholarly article, into the famous interpretative crux leading to the final 'Epitaph.' He then goes on to entice the reader into imagining Gray's process of poetic composition by printing seven cancelled or ultimately transformed stanzas.

In these notes he reveals more knowledge of American writing than might be expected. Of Longfellow's *Hiawatha,* he makes the point, which most Americans don't know, that the poem is "a decent and respectful attempt, more successful than is nowadays conceded, at an American epic." Of Tithonus, he points out that, granted one wish, "He thoughtlessly chose eternal life, not eternal youth," suggesting how crucial the selection of the exact word may be, and suggesting as well what an effective university teacher of poetry Amis would have made. He would have made a fine textual critic too, as is indicated in his locating a time-honored misprint in Charles Kingsley's "Song: When I Was a Greenhorn and Young." Now and then, like a conscientious teacher, he will quietly startle the reader-student with a sophisticated anti-romantic reminder that poetry is not photography and a poet is never on oath. Of Christina Rossetti's sensuous celebration of "Summer," full of precisely observed details, he is constrained to observe that it was "written in mid-January, in London." And commenting on Gerard Manley Hopkins's "In the Valley of the Elwy," he observes that two idiomatically odd passages exhibit Hopkins's "obsessive affectation of singularity." This offers an opportunity for his customary denigration of Poe as "the first bad poet in our language, as opposed to many who are merely no good." Vanity and egotism lie behind these attempts to write not like anyone else, and thus, finally, to ignore the public, if not actively to sod it.

His comments on Housman pay tribute to his unforgettable English teacher at City of London School, the Reverend C. J. Ellingham, from whom he learned that "you need not agree with a poem to value it or be moved by it." Something of that liberal spirit visits Amis's note on the nine poems of Auden he includes. Immensely fond of these poems, he can forgive the early ones their obscurity, but he now sees that the obscurity is interestingly "connected with his homosexuality," in an age when that had to be to a large degree unflaunted. Thus "secretiveness spreads out in his work to become a part of the style, an almost instinctive mystification." Hence Auden's greatness: "To make public poetry, to-be-published poetry out of a private language is to work under a handicap only a great poet could have overcome." That's an acute observation, but not all the notes are that sharp: some tiresomely wage Amis's war against stylish progressivism, Kipling-hatred, unidiomatic usage—he catches the luckless Margaret Drabble in an embarrassing idiomatic lapse—and the showy introduction of foreign languages into English poems. He even takes an opportunity to skewer war-skeptics and pacifists ("a progressive intelligentsia to whom there can be no such thing as a just feat of arms"). But these things merely add to the human interest of the anthology, and do not at all weaken its standing as one of Amis's most impressive works. Not the least impressive thing about it is its showing the way an intellect uses art in its own development, retaining as indispensable for a lifetime certain works which have been significant milestones on the way.

Throughout, his concern is for the reader, as always, and that is a concern even more palpable in *The Pleasure of Poetry*. This anthology is the fruit of an act unique in literary history. For the first time, an eminent man of letters presided over a poetry feature in a newspaper that would have to be designated proletarian, presenting five times a week a poem from the English-language repertory and providing a brief comment on it. Amis's poetry column lasted a year, from March 19, 1984, until March 15, 1985. Collected, these columns became *The Pleasure of Poetry*. It began at a drinks party, Amis remembers, when his friend Mike Molloy, editor of the *Daily Mirror* (circulation: over 3,000,000), astonished him by asking him if he'd like to serve as poetry editor. Part of the motive was to see how many people would respond to poetry that was understandable and that did not humiliate them. And part was to see what poems they would like the most. It was the sort of educational experiment that appealed to this talented ex-university teacher who now sometimes missed the classroom. "Dozens of letters," he says, "showed that it was not necessary to have been taught about Blake or Wordsworth or Anne Brontë or Housman, or even to have heard of them before, in order to appreciate them." Selecting the daily poems and recommending them in language refreshingly far from the usual critical jargon "turned out to be the most enjoyable job I ever had"—more enjoyable, notice, than writing novels, or criticism, or even restaurant reviews.

The *Daily Mirror* printed the column, headed "Kingsley Amis on Poetry" and accompanied by a smiling photo, on the same page as the comics, just before "Mirror Sport" and just after the TV schedule. Of course Amis had no trouble finding the poems. "A couple of days with . . . *The Faber Popular Reciter* gave me enough for the first weeks or months and I read every anthology by others that I could find, also a few dozen [volumes] of collected poems. I sent in batches of five or ten, enough for a week or a fortnight." Weren't you, I asked him, functioning as a sort of unconventional teacher of literature? He answered: "I didn't then or at any time since 1961 think of myself as a teacher of literature, though I wouldn't actually object to being so designated." The tone of the brief article he wrote to introduce this new feature is notably that of a teacher of, say, ordinary secondary-school students who have come to the detested subject "Poetry" with all the customary prejudices and who might be confused or repelled by complex sentences:

> Poetry is important. It is not a highbrow fad nor a youthful fun thing nor a tasteful amusement for old ladies.
>
> Poetry shows the human race asking and trying to answer those basic questions that are also at the root of religion:
>
> WHAT are we doing on this earth?
>
> HOW are we to live our lives?
>
> WHAT really matters?
>
> IS there anything that will help us overcome or put up with the darker side of our natures and our lives?
>
> Poetry is not a lot of pious sentiments dressed up in agreeable language.
>
> It can be as lively, painful, funny, bitter, tender, scathing or stirring as anything else in words.

He goes on to justify traditional poetic techniques, pointing out that rhyme and meter and other "sound effects" are there to make poetry fully expressive—more so than prose—and memorizable, and he can't resist observing that "most poetry now being produced is shapeless, rhymeless meterless nonsense. . . ."

(It has doubtless crossed Amis's mind that the bulk of contemporary poets are charlatans without any talent whatever, of whom Potter, in "Dear Illusion," is so representative as to win the big national poetry prize. Amis presents three sample poems by him. One is in free verse with 23 lines of varying length and no predication anywhere—just random words juxtaposed as if meaningful. Another is a portentous but incoherent "prose poem" mentioning *man, shell, sea, rock, sky, leaves,* and similar OK fixtures. Literate Americans may be reminded of the poem presented by Maya Angelou at the inauguration of President Clinton. The third example of Potter's work is a mock-vigorous eight-line attempt at a bold statement—which fails to state anything at all. Of course: Potter has nothing to say.)

This kind of "false poetry"—from BBC broadcasts down to reading in pubs and printings on T-shirts—is more and more persuading people that this is all there is, and, says Amis, "it is a depressing thought that there must be men and women in this country who have never been shown real poetry and have no idea what they are missing. From next Monday, readers of the *Daily Mirror*, at least, will no longer have to go without." And then a heartfelt conclusion, in italics: *"I think that this is a wonderfully bold and imaginative enterprise for a daily newspaper, and I am proud and delighted to have been chosen to set it going."* (Sensing the possibility of a disaster arising from misunderstanding, the editor has added at the end, "Please do not send YOUR poems for the time being.")

The style of Amis's introductory statement, simple and clear but without condescension, is that of a thoughtful, modest, un-snobbish educator, and it is the style of his daily commentaries on the poems. If a cliché will explain something better than an original phrase, he will, without anxiety, use the cliché. Commenting on Arnold's "To Marguerite," he writes, "Every man is an island, he says here," and elsewhere he explains that a standard poem for centuries was one in which the lover complains that "the object of his affection" ignores him. And at one point he uses *plus* to mean *and* in a thoroughly plebeian way. Aware that he's addressing readers not interested in fine points of taste or in literary contro-versies, here he is fairness itself towards poets he's usually skeptical about, like Plath, Dylan Thomas, John Ashbery, Ted Hughes, as well as Shelley, Hopkins, and even the despised Edgar Allan Poe. The reader's enjoyment, not high principle, is the object, after all. Dylan Thomas receives his due: of "Light Breaks Where No Sun Shines," Amis observes, "In almost everything Thomas wrote he created a particular kind of excitement no one else has matched, what seems a quite new sense that the realms of the imagination are infinite. . . . He must have attracted hundreds of thousands of people to poetry." For that, much posturing, thieving, and fraud may be forgiven. And faced with Plath's "The Moon and the Yew Tree," Amis is able to overcome his distaste for egotism and to say that although Plath's "subject is never anything but herself, . . . there is no doubt about her originality and curious power." And some of his comments on American poems are triumphs of generosity and the emotion appropriate to it. On July 4th, when he prints Emerson's "Concord Hymn," the word *salute,* rare in Amis's critical vocabulary, makes an impressive entrance:

> Concord was the village in Massachusetts where in 1775 the first engagement of the American War of Independence took place. In 1837 a granite obelisk was erected there and Emerson wrote this poem for the occasion. It is offered this month in salute to the United States of America and its people on their national day.

And its people: not necessary, just emotionally generous.

In his brief paragraph appended to each poem, he does not refrain from the sort of speculation which borders on gossip but which may entice readers to seek out more poetry. Thus on Housman's "The Recruit," he comments,

> Poems about battles and soldiering in general seem to have been written by almost all the Victorian poets. It has been suggested that this was an indirect way of working off sexual repression. However this might apply to Tennyson, for instance, it is certainly worth considering in the case of Housman, a bachelor don.

And he is careful to call readers' attention not just to the art of a given poem but to its uses—moral or intellectual or as a device for raising their morale. And there is a frequent effort to bridge the chasm between art and "most people," as in his comment on Rossetti's "Sudden Light," which begins, "I have been here before": "Here he captures the mysterious feeling of déjà vu that most people have experienced at some point in their lives." And sometimes his comment invites the reader to read more closely and critically, to think hard while reading, and to demand sense from poetry. About Longfellow's "Psalm of Life" he says of the stanza

> Lives of great men all remind us
> We can make our lives sublime,
> And, departing, leave behind us
> Footprints on the sands of time,

"those footprints have always bothered me a little. Footprints even in damp sand tend not to last long." Sometimes the echo of the B. Litt. thesis is heard, and one senses the fleeting image of a time when poetry was alive. About Alice Meynell's "Renouncement" he says, "Evidently Dante Gabriel Rossetti went round reciting it by heart to his friends, and Browning was quite bowled over."

But regardless of the poem he's commenting on, Amis seldom lets slip by an opportunity to hint his sympathy with ordinary people. He understands that his *Daily Mirror* readers represent myriads of the undistinguished and unnoticeable. Housman, he tells them, "could find the right words for what we have all seen and not noticed." And of Betjeman's complacent Second World War lady praying "In Westminster Abbey" both for the maximum destruction of Germans and the stability of her brokerage account, Amis notes that as well as satire the poem conveys "a horrible feeling that the lady is no worse than most of us." Throughout the year, he was careful to mark anniversaries and holidays with appropriate poems. For Christmas Day he could have gratified sophisticated readers by choosing Hardy's "The Oxen" or pleased conventional ones by printing some well-known carol. Instead, he gave his readers something closer to their own lives, Betjeman's "Christmas," with its comic but friendly specifications of the cynicisms and follies of a commercial Christmas in the city, emphasizing the spurious greetings, the phony bonhomie, the awful presents—but noting also the genuine, modest love prompting the gifts:

> . . . girls in slacks remember Dad,
> And oafish louts remember Mum

as they buy

> Bath salts and inexpensive scent
> And hideous tie so kindly meant.

but silly as it all is, vulgar and pathetic, it commemorates something quite serious, if easily overlooked,

> That God was Man in Palestine
> And lives to-day in Bread and Wine.

Amis's comment: "A splendid poem to express good wishes for Christmas and the New Year." For New Year's Day, he offers Tennyson's Wild-Bells stanzas from *In Memoriam,* and comments, with winning sympathy and informality, "Let us try to share his optimism." When he stepped down after the year's task was over, he felt regret but also immense happiness and pride that he had done his part to raise poetry, now fallen on bad times, to something like the popular status it not too long ago enjoyed. (Amis in the B. Litt. thesis: "When *In Memoriam* was published William [Morris] was sent out to get an advance copy, and the others stayed up until midnight waiting for him. On its arrival, Rossetti read out the entire poem . . . .") Amis had received thousands of letters of encouragement and praise, and he must have felt that he'd done exactly what he'd aimed at when John Mortimer told him that three years after the poetry column had closed down, a London taxi driver said that he missed it.

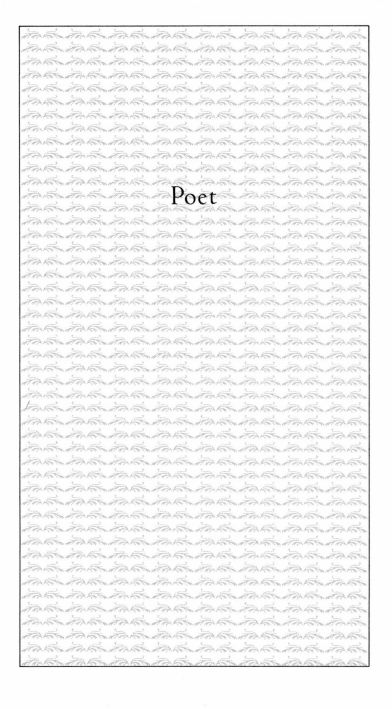

Poet

I T'S hard not to see Amis's own hand in the third-person jacket blurb for his *Collected Poems, 1944–1979*. It reports his conviction "that poetry is a higher art than fiction" and announces that "he started his career as a poet and has continued to write in that medium ever since." Yes, but it would be a mistake to assume that his poetic impulse has been artistically consistent or that from the outset he has written memorable poems.

With *Lucky Jim*, he found his novelist's voice immediately. Finding his poet's voice took him considerably longer. I don't mean a plausible voice appropriate to a certain kind of poem. As an accomplished mimic he could do that well from the beginning. I mean his own unique poetic voice, immediately identifiable as his and no one else's. The voice he finally released is one that accurately implies his attitudes and understandings without any artistic fakery or forcing. It is wholly original, deriving from no one, and it is a notable achievement.

Those only can be parodied who have achieved such a unique voice. By 1973, with Amis's own poetic method and tone firmly in his possession and well known to the public, Clive James could publish in the *New Statesman* for December 21, 1973, a parody of a poem about Dai Evans that Amis might have included in his group of poems about this cynical, sexually greedy Welsh layabout. It hardly needed to be presented as by "Kingsley Amiss," so widely enjoyed by this time was Amis's poetic voice:

What About You?

When Mrs Taflan Gruffydd-Lewis left Dai's flat
She gave her coiffe a pat
Having straightened carefully those nylon seams
Adopted to fulfil Dai's wicked dreams.
Evans didn't like tights.
He liked plump white thighs pulsing under thin skirts in
    packed pubs on warm nights.

That's that, then, thought Evans, hearing her Jag start,
And test-flew a fart.
Stuffing the wives of these industrial shags may be all
Very well, and *this* one was an embassy bar-room brawl
With Madame Nhu.
Grade A. But give them that fatal twelfth inch and they'll
    soon take their cue

To grab a yard of your large intestine or include your glans
Penis in their plans
For that Rich, Full Emotional Life you'd thus far ducked
So successfully.
Yes, Evans was feeling . . . Mucked-
up sheets recalled their scrap.
Thinking barbed thoughts in stanza form after shafting's a
    right sweat. Time for a nap.

That sort of thing would have been hard earlier, for Amis's earlier poems were themselves virtual unconscious parodies of someone else's voice, namely, Auden's.

At Oxford it was Larkin who introduced Amis to Auden's work. Larkin was an extravagant admirer, who later confessed that he bought an Audi because, as Andrew Motion reports his saying, "The name . . . reminds me of Auden." And watching Wimbledon once, he noticed that Boris Becker looked remarkably like the young Auden. Noting that the poems of Robert Herrick seemed relatively neglected in his anthologies, I once asked Amis, "Why are you down on Herrick?" He answered, forcefully if perhaps illogically, "Because he's not Auden."

As critic William H. Pritchard has said, in Amis's early poems there's a lot of Auden but very little Amis. The Amis would have to wait until he had mastered the art of inviting the social critic and satirist to join the poet. The early poems exhibit numerous Audenesque twitches: for example, the human body seen in topographical terms, or vice versa:

> Still flows your northern river like a pulse,
> Carrying blood to bodies at the poles.
>> "Letter to Elisabeth"

or denominating an addressee as "Stranger":

> So, stranger, when you come here to unpack, . . .
> Expect from me nothing but a false wish
> That, going, you ignore all other partings,
> And find no ghosts that growl or whinny of
> Kisses from nowhere, negligible tears.
>> "Bed and Breakfast"

Sometimes there is what looks like technological showing-off:

> Kolster and Dunmore made a remarkable valve
> Which would bind forever the sense of the plunging
>> wave . . .

*   *   *

> Meanwhile the radiation sprang from the tentative rod,
> Adored by the hymn of the mains singing like ladies . . .
>> "Radar"

169

Early, he's fond of quasi-didactic attempts at general truth, registered openly in the first-person plural:

> For life, too feminine, always insists
> On smiling when we want to be serious,
> Has no sense of the cinema . . . .
>> "Retrospect"

His early talent is for echoing Auden poems that deploy general
truths in aid of maintaining morale:

AUDEN:　The sense of danger must not disappear:
　　　　The way is certainly both short and steep,
　　　　However gradual it looks from here;
　　　　Look if you like, but you will have to leap.
　　　　　　　　　　　　　　　　　"Leap Before You Look"

AMIS:　　That horse whose rider fears to jump will fall,
　　　　Riflemen miss if orders sound unsure;
　　　　They only are secure who seem secure;
　　　　Who lose their voice, lose all.
　　　　　　　　　　　　　　　　　"Masters"

In many of these early poems there's a tolerance of obscurity, if
not a positive hankering after it. Indeed, for a few years at the
beginning, Amis produced the kinds of poems he finally came to
deplore: university stuff aimed not at the general reader but at
clever friends and colleagues who were wild for Auden, Eliot, and
Donne. There is thus something resembling exclusivism, even
snobbery, in these early poems. He is taking himself seriously. The
mocking, self-critical sardonic "What About You?" vein he has not
yet located, secured, and exploited. But once, in 1947, he made a
little tentative progress towards something different in the poem
"Belgian Winter." Here the Auden influence has been tamed by a
sense of life rather than literature, needless metaphor has been
eschewed, and a successful poem has resulted. (The scene is near
Brussels, with the war in progress):

170

*   *   *

From my window stretches the earth, containing wrecks:
The burrowing tank, the flat grave, the
Lorry with underside showing, like a dead rabbit.

*   *   *

But there are people here, unable to understand,
Randy for cigarettes, moving hands too
Jerky to move in love; their women matrons, their
      daughters
Fanatically guarded or whores with lovely teeth.

*   *   *

the pubs

Like railway buffets, bare and impersonal.
Smiles exclude the hypothesis of starving, but
The conqueror is advised to keep to the boulevards.

But this was an uncerain way-station in Amis's progress towards
his authentic voice. He found it beyond any doubt in the early
1950s as he worked on the poems in his second collection, *A Case
of Samples* (1956). Abandoning the high poetic and the portentous,
he now embraced the mode, as Pritchard has pointed out, of *vers de
société.* In his Introduction to *The New Oxford Book of Light Verse,* he
describes it as

> a kind of realistic verse that is close to some of the interests of the
> novel: men and women among their fellows, seen as members of a
> group or class in a way that emphasizes manners, social forms,
> amusements, fashion (from millinery to philosophy), topicality,
> even gossip, all these treated in a bright, perspicuous style.

That is what he turned to, and that is where he found his voice,
informal, anti-poetic, unexpectedly frank, satiric, urban—emi-
nently "civic," an appropriate instrument for the delivery of
"barbed thoughts."

It would be hard to point to one poem as marking a definite
transition from the old to the new style, but "Nocturne" can
illustrate the new down-to-earth analytic impulse. Now, instead of

171

beginning with a general truth ("That horse whose rider fears to jump will fall"), he begins empirically with a novelist's particulars of time, place, and characters, which he scrutinizes in order finally to earn a generalization:

> Under the winter street-lamps, near the bus-stop,
> Two people with nowhere to go fondle each other,
> Writhe slowly in the entrance to a shop.
> In the intervals of watching them, a sailor
> Yaws about with an empty beer-flagon,
> Looking for something good to smash it on.
>
> *Mere animals:* on this the Watch Committee
> And myself seem likely to agree;
> But all this fumbling about, this wasteful
> Voiding of sweat and breath—is that *animal?*
>
> Nothing so sure and economical.
>
> These keep the image of another creature
> In crippled versions, cocky, drab and stewed;
> What beast holds off its paw to gesture,
> Or gropes towards being understood?

(And in the final four lines, he has an opportunity to honor Wilfred Owen's technique of near-rhyming. Once Owen discovered it, "overnight," says Amis, "English poetry came into possession of thousands of fresh rhymes.")

The same dynamics characterize "A Bookship Idyll," which, by means of data and examples, works towards the general truth that

> Women are really much nicer than men:
> No wonder we like them.

The poem is a triumph in Amis's authentic style, as anthologists seem to recognize: they generally ignore the early poems and, like friend Larkin compiling *The Oxford Book of Twentieth-Century English Verse,* begin their Amis selection with this one:

172

Between the GARDENING and the COOKERY
    Comes the brief POETRY shelf;
By the Nonesuch Donne, a thin anthology
    Offers itself.

Critical, and with nothing else to do,
    I scan the Contents page,
Relieved to find the names are mostly new,
    No one my age.

Like all strangers, they divide by sex:
    Landscape near Parma
Interests a man, so does *The Double Vortex,*
    So does *Rilke and Buddha.*

"I travel, you see," "I think" and "I can read"
    These titles seem to say;
But *I Remember You, Love is My Creed,*
    Poem for J.,

The ladies' choice, discountenance my patter
    For several seconds;
From somewhere in this (as in any) matter
    A moral beckons.

Should poets bicycle-pump the human heart
    Or squash it flat?
Man's love is of man's life a thing apart;
    Girls aren't like that.

We men have got love well weighed up; our stuff
    Can get by without it.
Women don't seem to think that's good enough;
    They write about it,

And the awful way their poems lay them open
    Just doesn't strike them.

> Women are really much nicer than men:
>> No wonder we like them.
>
> Deciding this, we can forget those times
>> We sat up half the night
> Chockfull of love, crammed with bright thoughts,
>> names, rhymes,
> And couldn't write.

He's now secure enough in what he's doing to rely on natural, demotic diction (*patter, squash, stuff, awful*) and to quite forgo the grand, like *inflate,* in favor of the precise and the low, like *bicycle-pump.*

And now characters begin to populate the poems: Balbus, the horrible academic,

> Jerking and twitching as he walks,
> Neighing and hooting as he talks;

Constant Angst, "the art critic," and Old Major Courage; Buck, the schoolboy pederast, and Ralph, his strictly Platonic counterpart; and Sam Baines, the swinish local business magnate who bankrolls a civic university which, surprisingly, learns to equal Baines in its capacity for corruption and swindling. Next, Amis's search for interesting particulars prompts him to enter poems himself in his own erotic character:

Sight Unseen

> As I was waiting for the bus
>> A girl came up the street,
> Delectable as double-plus
>> At seven hundred feet.
>
> Her head was high, her step was free,
>> Her face a lyric blur;

Her waist was narrow, I could see,
    But not the rest of her.

At fifty feet I watched her stop,
    Bite at a glove, then veer
Aside into some pointless shop
    Never to reappear.

This happens every bloody day:
    They about-turn, they duck
Into their car and drive away,
    They hide behind a truck.

Look, if they knew me, well and good,
    There might be cause to run;
Or even saw me—understood;
    No. Not a peep. Not one.

Love at first sight—by this we mean
    A stellar entrant thrown
Clear on the psyche's radar-screen,
    Recognized before known.

All right: things work the opposite
    Way with the poles reversed;
It's galling, though, when girls omit
    To switch the set on first

But the glib erotic expert proves as liable to feelings of guilt as
anyone else:

Nothing to Fear

All fixed: early arrival at the flat
Lent by a friend, whose note says *Lucky sod;*
Drinks on the tray; the cover-story pat
And quite uncheckable; her husband off
Somewhere with all the kids till six o'clock

175

(Which ought to be quite long enough);
And all worth while: face really beautiful,
Good legs and hips, and as for breasts—my God.
What about guilt, compunction, and such stuff?
I've had my fill of all that cock;
It'll wear off, as usual.

Yes, all fixed. Then why this slight trembling,
Dry mouth, quick pulse-rate, sweaty hands,
As though she were the first? No, not impatience,
Nor fear of failure, thank you, Jack.
Beauty, they tell me, is a dangerous thing,
Whose touch will burn, but I'm asbestos, see?
All worth while—it's a dead coincidence
That sitting here, a bag of glands
Tuned up to concert pitch, I seem to sense
A different style of caller at my back,
As cold as ice, but just as set on me.

Two poems in *A Look Round the Estate* (1967) apply skepticism, humor, and anger to the normally dignified disciplines of teleology and Christian apologetics. The first, "The Huge Artifice: an interim assessment," treats the created world and the things that happen in it the way a literary critic would review a long novel. The critic finds it disappointing, not just in art, but in poetic, or any other kind of justice:

. . . First: what there is of plot
In thin, repetitive, leaning far too much
On casual meetings, parties, fights and such,
With that excessive use of coincidence
Which betrays authorial inexperience.

But if defective as an artist, the Creator is fatally indifferent to decency and fairness:

                              . . . crimes
        Are paid for never or a thousand times,
        . . . the gentle come to grief—all these are forced
        Into scenes, dialogue, comment, and endorsed
        By the main action, manifesting there
        An inhumanity beyond despair.

At about the same time—the mid-1960s—he was working on *The Anti-Death League,* another heartfelt cry against what he has stigmatized, in an essay on Waugh, as "the cruelty and arbitrariness at the heart of the universe." To one character in the novel, Max Hunter, is ascribed the brutally funny Amis poem "To a Baby Born Without Limbs." (The thalidomide scandal had surfaced in the early 1960s.) The poem (I have set right some intentional errors required by the plot) is sent anonymously to William Ayscue, Chaplain, whose job is precisely that of rationalizing inexplicable evil:

        This is just to show you who's boss around here.
        It'll keep you on your toes, so to speak,
        Make you put your best foot forward, so to speak,
        And give you something to turn your hand to, so to speak.
        You can face up to it like a man,
        Or snivel and blubber like a baby.
        That's up to you. Nothing to do with Me.
        If you take it in the right spirit,
        You can have a bloody marvelous life,
        With the great rewards courage brings,
        And the beauty of accepting your LOT.
        And think how much good it'll do your Mum and Dad,
        And your Grans and Gramps and the rest of the shower,
        To be stopped being complacent.
        Make sure they baptize you, though,
        In case some murdering bastard
        Decides to put you away quick,

Which would send you straight to LIMB-O, ha ha ha.
But just a word in your ear, if you've got one.
Mind you DO take this in the right spirit,
And keep a civil tongue in your head about Me.
Because if you DON'T,
I've got plenty of other stuff up My sleeve,
Such as leukemia and polio,
(Which incidentally you're welcome to any time,
Whatever spirit you take this in.)
I've given you one love-pat, right?
You don't want another.
So watch it, Jack.

Ayscue's reaction to this poem testifies to its success.

> Ayscue read it through three times. Then he went to his ward-
> robe . . . and took a bottle of Scotch out from among his foot-
> wear. He swallowed half a tooth-glassful neat in two goes, the first
> drink he had had before noon for over ten years.

And while in this I Hate Him mood, Amis turned his attention to
the Son of this all-powerful monster. The result was "New Approach Needed." This taxes Jesus with such inexperience of actual
human life that his maxims and panaceas are worthless. Next time
you come amongst us, he is told,

>   . . . what about a go
> At love, marriage, children?
> All good, but bringing some
> Risk of remorse and pain
> And fear of an odd sort:
> A sort one should, again,
> Feel, not just hear about,
> To be qualified as
> A human-race expert.
> On local life, we trust

The resident witness,
Not the royal tourist.

        *   *   *

So, next time . . .
. . . get some service in,
Jack, long before you start
Laying down the old law:
If you want to then.
Tell your Dad that from me.

It seems inevitable that Amis's long familiarity with Wales would find a place in his poems. It finds a significantly unromantic place in the dozen poems he groups under the title *The Evans Country*. It is as if he were exhibiting, with due amusement and affection, that side of Wales left unilluminated by emotion and rhapsody, by, that is, Dylan Thomas and his like. The hero of these poems, the lower-middle-class Dai Evans, is just a little less awful than the one in Clive James's parody. But he's never uninteresting, depicted as he is by the eye and hand of a satiric-moral novelist-poet with a soft spot for shrewd near-proletarians. Dai works in an office (unspecified), but his real work is getting girls, by deception, if possible—more fun that way. He is uniformly contemptuous of the girls he gets and the wives he enjoys in their husbands' absence, and in every human relation he is instinctively dishonest and selfish. His only virtue is persistence.

We are to infer that Dai's town is named Aberdarcy, and that it embraces or borders on the suburbs or areas of St. Asaph's, Langwell, Pendydd, Llansili Beach, Brynbwrla, and such. (One can sense the mind of the novelist working, delighting in making up plausible place-names.) Dai first enters the scene in the main square of Aberdarcy, within whose appalling commerical-"modern" architecture and in whose bad restaurants he prosecutes a several-week-long pursuit of one Mrs. Rhys. The reader gathers that it does not turn out very well. The quality of Dai's love is mirrored in the quality of the setting, and in explaining, Amis produces one of the best-written quatrains of the twentieth century:

> The journal of some bunch of architects
> Named this the worst town center they could find;
> But how disparage what so well reflects
> Permanent tendencies of heart and mind?

That is Ruskin and Morris brought up to date, the sense that artistic context powerfully influences behavior and understanding. And architectural squalor is precisely what Dai and Mrs. Rhys, as well as the rest of us, deserve, the only kind of setting appropriate to our shrivelled moral and artistic sensitivities:

> All love demands a witness: something "there"
> Which it yet makes part of itself. These two
> Might find Carlton House Terrace, St Mark's Square,
> A bit on the grand side. What about you?

In other poems we see Dai studying the schoolgirls, who, if now well below legal age, will come on soon enough. And we witness Dai making a backyard bonfire of some of his pornography, carefully saving out the good stuff. Sunbathing at Llansili Beach, he's aware that he's not the man he was, for now he must put on his glasses to appraise the girls. The form of "A two-piece with a fair lot in it" is clear once he's got his lenses in place. Now he leaps up, as of old, approaches, and "Hallo. Care for a smoke?" Moral:

> Your look/do ratio doesn't change.
> All that might is your visual range.

Serving as a judge of a beauty contest at Maunders (Amis once judged a real one at Mumbles), Dai is taken by the ripe figure of Miss Clydach, but he votes against her to win Mrs. Town Clerk's approval so that he can take her out. Attending his father's funeral, Dai plays the grieving son satisfactorily, but, the ceremony finished, he rushes to a pub phone:

> "Hello, pet. Alone? Good. It's me.
> Ah now, who did you think it was?
> Well, come down the Bush and find out.
> You'll know me easy, because
> I'm wearing a black tie, love."

Sometimes comfort takes precedence over even lust:

> Hearing how tourists, dazed with reverence,
> Looked through sunglasses at the Parthenon,
> Dai thought of that cold night outside the Gents
> When he touched Dilys up with his gloves on.

Finally, at 6:30 p.m., after

> A fearsome thrash with Mrs No-holds-barred
> (Whose husband's in his surgery till 7),

Dai decides to stay home this one night, eating a simple supper washed down with only a couple of bottles of light ale and watching TV. He needs the rest.

Moving on through the *Collected Poems*, one understands the anger at Nashville and Vanderbilt that occasioned the poem "South," but although it contains some accurate urban observation and telling mimicry (*"You blind? Can't you see they inferior?"*), it lacks irony and subtlety, achieving high moral purpose but little poetry. The very next poem illustrates Amis's greater talent for elegy and the theme of loss than for rebuke. And from here on his poems seem to turn increasingly autobiographical. "Bobby Bailey" is like a 24-line act of memory, recovering the boyhood fun of just dropping in at Bobby's house on Norbury Avenue (very near the boy Amis's house):

What super fun to just turn up, and find him
    Sprawled on the playroom floor,

Toppling West Kents, Carabineers, 5th Lancers
    With a mad marble-barrage,
Doling out Woodbines, Tizer and eclairs in
    The loft above the garage,

Or mouthing *Shitface!* at his sister Janet,
    Vision so rarely seen,
Slightly moustached, contemptuous, fine-featured,
    Full-breasted, and sixteen.

Fun to turn up . . .

And that is emphasized: turning up freely, without notice, instead of the adult necessity of planning, invitation, formality, anxiety. But the Baileys moved away, and since then there's been no contact between Bobby and Kingsley.

Of course. I know that, every year, some people
    Simply get up and go
Too far for you to see, much less drop in on,
    Less yet stay with. I know

"The past" is a good name for what's all over;
    You can't, in fact, return
To what isn't a place. It does sound like an
    Easy lesson to learn.

But still, just turning up will remain an image of Eden, forever both unrecoverable and unforgettable, with the power of souring by contrast every subsequent adult arrangement. As Amis says in "Lovely," a skeptical comment on Walter de la Mare's "Farewell" ("Look thy last on all things lovely / Every hour"),

The best time to see things lovely
    Is in youth's primordial bliss,

not later, when it's possible every hour to feel death drawing nearer. In a companion poem, "Shitty," Amis comically deplores the disappearance of the once beautiful and the deterioration of taste since de la Mare's time, the enshrining of soccer stars, the ubiquity of vicious football crowds, as well as

> German tourists, plastic roses,
>   Face of Mao and face of Che,

not to mention "Women wearing curtains, blankets." How, the implication is, could the "lovely" even be located any more?

As one expects, the literary past is never distant from Amis's poems. In "Peacefully," the remembered poem is "Verses on the Death of Dr. Swift," with its disclosure of the secret pleasure people feel when they know it's you that's died, not they:

> "You saw old Kingsley's gone?"—"Christ!
>   I hadn't heard he was ill."—"No age
>   To speak of, was he?" And the whole crew
>   Try to conceal their glee that this
>   Time it still isn't them.
> "Bad enough anyway, of course,
>   But one gathers he dropped off quite peacefully."

And Housman's "1887," his celebration of Victoria's Golden Jubilee, ironically haunts Amis's "Ode to Me," an address to himself on his fiftieth anniversary. Housman's poem is one of his all-time favorites: he includes it in *The Amis Anthology*, *The Faber Popular Reciter*, and *The Pleasure of Poetry*. It extols the bravery of the English common soldier in his sacrifice abroad for the Empire and ends with this advice to the living:

> Get you the sons your fathers got
>   And God will save the Queen.

Amis's view is less hopeful, for he observes what's happened

After a whole generation
Of phasing out education,
Throwing the past away,
Letting the language decay,

so that soon

it wouldn't make much odds
To the poor semi-sentient sods
Shuffling around England then
That they've lost what made them men.

But as things grow inexorably worse, there's still satisfaction knowing that one is old enough to have enjoyed some decency, wit, and
pleasure:

So bloody good luck to you, mate,
That you weren't born too late
For at least a chance of happiness,
Before unchangeable crappiness
Spreads over all the land.
Be glad you're fifty—and
That you got there while things were nice,
In a world worth looking at twice.
So here's wishing you many more years,
But not all that many. Cheers!

The narrative poem of some length is one of the more lamenta-
ble casualties of Modernism. In "A Reunion," Amis shows what
can still be done with it. Is it just my having also been a junior
officer in an army that makes me so fond of this poem about a
Second World War unit's gathering thirty years later? I think not.
The poem is magnificently written, a triumphant mediation between the facts—such a gathering actually took place—and the
artistic needs of the poem. In *Memoirs*, he rounds off his chapter
"The Army" thus:

One day in 1975 or so I got a letter addressed to "Dear Bill" from someone I remembered well and with liking as Lance-Corporal Waddington, inviting me to a reunion. . . . The venue was one of those assembly-room places off Edgware Road. . . . Reunions are dodgy undertakings, like formal dinners or luncheons in that they can suddenly set you wondering if anybody at all among those present is enjoying himself to the smallest degree. . . . But of course I turned up, out of curiosity I said to myself, but also to see others I had liked besides Les Waddington.

That hope was to a large extent dashed. Most of those he'd liked weren't there, and of course all looked so much older that the effect was grotesque.

And they were duller, too, most of them. The shine and cheerfulness of youth can appear at first blush very like real vitality, even wit. Time will lay bare the disappointing truth. . . .

Turning this into a formal poem 200 lines long without at every point shouting "This is a poem!" took all Amis's technical skill. He could easily have written it in blank verse, but that would have been very little fun. Instead, he writes it in 25 eight-line stanzas, each consisting of two generally octosyllabic quatrains rhyming rigorously *abab*, but rhyming not at all intrusively or even always noticeably, thanks to an occasional near-rhyme and the conversational word-order, as well as the colloquial, sometimes army, language. There is an entire absence of such poeticisms as earnest metaphor and "suggestion," and not an Audenism is to be heard. Here's the way Amis describes former Major MacClure, once adjutant of the unit:

> you could say
> That Sandy MacClure was a real
> Panjandrum of shits in his day,
> But the bugger could get you to laugh:
> Killing take-offs of his mates,
> The trip-wires he laid for the Staff,
> That truck-load of Yank cigarettes

(rhyming with *mates*). Other ex-soldiers Amis remembers include

> Slosher Perkins, disciple of Marx,
> With his pamphlets and posters; Burnett
> (Was he one of the company clerks?),
> The booziest sod of the lot;
> Young Taylor, obstreperous enough
> In spite of that choirboyish look;
> Shy little Corporal Clough,
> Who would talk about Shelley and Blake.

And as Amis makes his way to

> the Allied Services Club,
> 6 Upper Greenhill Street,
> (Opposite Farringdon Tube),

on a Friday,

> any time after 6 p. m.,

the wartime scene comes back, what it was "then":

> Then farmyards and cobbled roads
> Full of sun, fresh fruit, village wells,
> Tents pitched in the leaf-strewn woods,
> Slow crossing of iced-up canals,
> Those seasons, that mutable scene
> Trodden through in the end—all that
> Plus liters of lager and wine
> And a sniff or so at the frat.

(He explains *frat* in a note, necessary only for those not male and below the age of sixty-five: "'Fraternization' between Allied troops and German nationals, including females, was forbidden by order

of General Eisenhower in 1944. Phrases like 'a piece of frat' soon
became current.") Then, up some rather tacky stairs and into the
meeting-room to confront—total strangers, largely:

> there   —
> Was Jim, with a grey moustache
> And a belly, but still—"Good God!"
> I said, "you look just the same,
> You treacherous, miserable sod!"
> "I'm sorry," he said—"what's the name?"

Former boozehound Tom Burnett is now totally on ginger ale, his
liver having gone, and Burnett supplies news about Clough:

> "Harry Clough? Nice fellow. He's dead."

But Amis is not entirely disappointed. He finds

> The chap who had been
> Young Taylor quite well preserved.

After drinks and snacks there are speeches,

> On things like the lately deceased
> And how lucky we were to be there.

Ex-Major MacClure now arrives, and Amis asks him about the
absent Nicholls.

> (A privilege granted to few
> Is meeting a pratt on the scale
> Of Nicholls: by common consent
> A nitwit not fit to shift shit;
> Whether more of a bastard or cunt
> Views varied, one has to admit.)

Amis recalls MacClure formerly ridiculing Nicholls, but now he shocks Amis by announcing that he and Nicholls meet now and then for a drink. Appalled, Amis reminds MacClure of his forcefully saying once that if he ever, ever drank with Nicholls he would deserve to have his head examined.

> "Oh yes?" said MacClure. "Well, you know
> How it is—you exaggerate. And
> It was all a long time ago . . . ."

And then an instructive humiliation for Amis:

> "One thing about Nicholls, Bill,
> He always stuck up for you,
> And you needed a spot of goodwill."

Now the reunion breaks up, and it's time for Amis to ruminate on its meaning:

> What had brought us together before
> Was over, no doubt about that;
> What had held us together was more
> Than, whether you liked it or not,
> Going after a single aim,
> One procedure laid down from above;
> In their dozens, no two the same,
> Small kinds and degrees of love.
>
> And that was quite natural then,
> When to do what we had to do
> Showed us off perfectly, when
> We were not so much young as new,
> With some shine still on us, unmarked
> (At least only mildly frayed),
> When everything in us worked,
> And no allowances made.

So, when one of us had his leave stopped,
Was awarded a dose of the clap
Or an extra guard, or was dropped
Up to his ears in the crap,
Or felt plain bloody browned off,
He never got left on his own:
The others had muscle enough
To see that he soldiered on.

And finally, the realization that if they did escape death once, they're not going to escape it this time:

Disbandment has come to us
As it comes to all who grow old;
Demobilized now, we face
What we faced when we first enrolled.

The only defense against despair is the same discipline and pride that, on parade, countered despair back then:

Stand still in the middle rank!
See you show them a touch of pride!—
Left-right, left-right, bags of swank—
On the one-man pass-out parade.

(That, as is doubtless obvious, is my favorite Amis poem, and my favorite passage in it is

We were not so much young as new, . . .
When everything in us worked,
And no allowances made.)

"A Reunion" could serve as a model for the redemption of contemporary poetry and its return to its rightful audience, for it combines the human interest, pace, and suspense of narrative with the formality and high art of poetic technique. But no one seems to have noticed.

"A Reunion" is not the only product of Amis's turn in the late 1970s to acts of wry reminiscence and considerations of the past in relation to aging and the inevitable future. A minor English publishing event in 1977 was the appearance of *My Oxford*, a collection of reminiscences by John Betjeman, Angus Wilson, Nigel Nicolson, John Mortimer, Antonia Fraser, Martin Amis, and others. Some of the older graduates recalled such prewar pleasures as champagne luncheons in their rooms, presided over by a college servant, and upper-middle-class high-jinks associated with sneaking in late, spending money on the latest outlandish male fashions, acting in the Oxford University Dramatic Society, punting on the river, and generally treating Oxford as just another setting for the life of privilege. Amis's reaction was the two-part poem "Their Oxford."

The first part, an account of Oxford revisited, reveals how sadly the place has deteriorated in beauty and seriousness in the mere thirty years since Amis's time there. The Randolph Hotel, once a haunt of parents and fiancées, a place where dons took their favorite students for flirtatious luncheons and dinners, has sunk to accepting tours of traveling foreigners whose talk is too loud and who call, in the bar, for ice in malt whisky. Formerly, even the workaday parts of the city had a self-respecting life of their own. Before, the Cornmarket was somewhat like a market,

> Where men in long top-coats would snort and scratch,
> Meat-market porters gulp their morning break,
> And stall-boys jostle . . . .

But now

> you catch
> The surge and thunder of a discothèque.

After this Eliotic look at the way Oxford has changed, Amis turns to his experience there, and focusing on his entire lack of familiarity, through poverty and pride, with the glamorous, Zuleika Dobson, Evelyn Waugh life of expensive gaiety and charm, he wonders if today even that style can persist. In one of his very best-written passages, he asks if the classy Commem. Ball still occurs as a main source of excitement for students not like Amis:

> Do costly girls still throng the chequered lawn,
> All bosom and bright hair, as they did then,
> And laugh and dance and chatter until dawn
> With peacock-minded, donkey-voiced young men?

But a single rotting college barge in the river where there was once a spic-and-span dozen suggests the answer: even the Oxford "that I hardly knew" has suffered a sad change. Amis used to scorn that rich Oxford, while at the same time coveting it mildly,

> but at this remove,
> When no one here cares how it used to be
> Except the old, can I still disapprove?

Distanced now, he concludes that any part of the past, no matter how silly and worthless, looks better than the present. And the future.

He ends the *Collected Poems* with "Farewell Blues," implicit homage to both Hardy's "Friends Beyond" and Betjeman's "Dorset." Hardy's poem engaged in a roll-call of locals of various social stations now laid away past caring:

> William Dewy, Tranter Reuben, Farmer Ledlow late at
>   plough,
>   Robert's kins, and John's, and Ned's,
> And the Squire, and Lady Susan, lie in Mellstock churchyard
>   now!

Betjeman's poem similarly suggests the social equality of the grave, which has the power to equate rural with urban, simple with sophisticated, and to render absurd and pathetic all social strivings:

> Rime Intrinsica, Fontmell Magna, Sturminster Newton, and
>   Melbury Bubb,
> Whist upon whist upon whist upon whist drive, in Institute,
>   Legion and Social Club.
> Horny hands that hold the aces that this morning held
>   the plough—
> While Tranter Reuben, T. S. Eliot, H. G. Wells and Edith
>   Sitwell lie in Mellstock Churchyard now.

(Betjeman adds a note: "The names . . . are put in not out of malice or satire but merely for their euphony.")

Amis's redaction of these two poems eliminates both the social-equality theme and the social pathos to engage in angry regret at the replacement of genuine jazz with its bogus successor bearing, impudently, the same name. Now the churchyards are the trade-labels of the old 78s that used to delight Amis and Larkin. The instruments have changed, the discipline has vanished, and the conventions are now irrecoverable:

*   *   *

> Dead's the note we loved that swelled within us, made us
>   gasp and stare,
> Simple joy and simple sadness thrashing the astounded air,
> What replaced them no one asked for, but it turned up
>   anyhow,
> And Coleman Hawkins, Johnny Hodges, Bessie Smith and
>   Pee Wee
>   Russell lie in Okeh churchyard now,

Thus Amis completes the cycle, returning near the end to moments of young delight and to things as they once were. It is not every contemporary poet whose works so neatly enact the passages of an actual life, from boyish wonder and comedy and outrage to mature guilt and regret, and finally to pained but courageous acceptance of what must be.

His rejection of Modernism, his sense of its unjustified perverse interruption of the course of English literature, with attendant social divisiveness, has earned him a reputation as a sort of unreconstructed late-Victorian who has outlived his proper moment, and with his refusal to fly, drive, use a word-processor, or have a fax machine in the house, he might be called, now that Betjeman is gone, The Last Victorian. Some have come to see him as a mere philistine, pigheadedly set against the subtleties of modern poetry, fiction, music, and painting. But Barbara Everett has written to clear the air:

> The word "philistine" is always hard to handle, and there are self-evident ways in which it simply cannot be applied to a man who has spent his life in literature: writing and thinking, teaching and lecturing, reviewing and caring for books and manuscripts . . . .

And we may wonder whether a man is properly called a philistine who seems to have read more Pound and Joyce than his detractors have read Newbolt, Kipling, Betjeman, and Edwin Muir.

What to call him then? Novelist? Poet? Literary and social critic? These terms are all too limiting. How about Man of Letters?

Sources

(Place of publication is London unless otherwise indicated. *Salwak:* Dale Salwak, ed., *Kingsley Amis in Life and Letters*, 1990.)

Amis, Kingsley (ed.), *The Amis Anthology*, 1988
———— *The Amis Collection: Selected Non-Fiction, 1954–1990*, 1990
———— *The Anti-Death League*, 1966
———— *Collected Poems, 1944–1979*, New York, 1979
———— *Collected Short Stories*, 1987
———— (with Robert Conquest), *The Egyptologists*, 1965
———— "English Non-Dramatic Poetry, 1850–1900, and the Victorian Reading Public" (B. Litt. thesis)
———— (ed.), *The Faber Popular Reciter*, 1978
———— *The Folks That Live on the Hill*, 1990
———— (ed., with James Cochrane), *The Great British Songbook*, 1986
———— *I Like It Here*, 1958
———— "Is the Travel-Book Dead?," *Spectator*, June 17, 1955
———— *Jake's Thing*, 1978
———— *Lucky Jim*, 1954
———— *Memoirs*, 1991
———— (ed.), *The Oxford Book of Light Verse*, 1978
———— *The Old Devils*, 1986
———— *On Drink*, 1972
———— (ed.), *The Pleasure of Poetry, From His Daily Mirror Column*, 1990
———— *The Riverside Villas Murder*, 1973
———— *Rudyard Kipling*, 1975
———— *The Russian Girl*, 1992

———— *Stanley and the Women,* 1984

———— *Take a Girl Like You,* 1960

Auden, W. H., *Collected Poems,* ed. Edward Mendelson, New York, 1976

Bennett, Catherine, "My Life and Silly Old Sods," *Guardian,* Feb. 25, 1991

Blunden, Edmund, *Poems of Many Years,* 1957

Carpenter, Humphrey, *W. H. Auden: A Biography,* 1981

Conarroe, Joel, "Nasty Boy," *New York Times Book Review,* Sept. 8, 1991

Everett, Barbara, "Kingsley Amis: Devils and Others," in *Salwak,* pp. 89–99

Fussell, Paul, "Kingsley, As I Know Him," in *Salwak,* pp. 18–23

Gross, John, *The Rise and Fall of the Man of Letters: Aspects of English Literary Life Since 1800,* 1969; 1991

James, Clive, *Other Passports: Poems, 1958–1985,* 1986

Johnson, Paul, "Is Your Journey Really Necessary, Professor?," *Spectator,* Sept. 7, 1991

Johnson, Samuel, *Lives of the English Poets,* ed. G. B. Hill (3 vols.), Oxford, 1905

Kirkup, James, *I, Of All People,* 1988

Larkin, Philip, *Collected Poems,* ed. Anthony Thwaite, 1988

Miller, Karl, *Authors,* Oxford, 1989

Mortimer, John, Interview with Kingsley Amis, *Sunday Times,* Sept. 18, 1988

Motion, Andrew, *Philip Larkin: A Writer's Life,* 1993

Phelps, Gilbert, "The 'Awfulness' of Kingsley Amis," in *Salwak,* pp. 65–75

Pritchard, William H., "Entertaining Amis," in *Salwak,* pp. 173–82

Ritchie, Harry, "An Outrageous Talent," in *Salwak,* pp. 183–87

Scannell, Vernon, Introduction to *Elected Friends: Poems for and about Edward Thomas,* ed. Anne Harvey, 1991

Spurling, Hilary, Review of *The Russian Girl, Daily Telegraph,* April 18, 1992

Stannard, Martin, *Evelyn Waugh: No Abiding City,* 1992

About the Author

Paul Fussell was born in California and educated at Pomona College and Harvard. From 1943 to 1946 he served as a lieutenant in the American infantry. He has lived in France, Germany, and England, and traveled widely in Europe and the Middle East. His books of literary and cultural criticism and social history include *Poetic Meter and Poetic Form, Samuel Johnson and The Life of Writing, The Great War and Modern Memory, Abroad: British Literary Travelling Between the Wars, Thank God for the Atom Bomb and Other Essays,* and *Wartime: Understanding and Behavior in the Second World War.* He has taught English at Connecticut College; Rutgers; the University of Heidelberg; King's College, London; and the University of Pennsylvania. He is married to journalist Harriette Behringer and lives in Philadelphia.

Index

George II, 110
Gershwin, George, 118
Getty, J. Paul, 125
Gilbert, W. S., 144
Gilbert & Sullivan, 23
Gissing, George, 46
Glendinning, Victoria, 47
Golding, William, 83
Goldwater, Barry M., 6
Gollancz, Victor, 83
Goodman, Benny, 23
Gosse, Edmund, 46, 47
"Gran," 21
Graves, Robert, 32, 46, 84, 87
Gray, Simon, 60–61
Gray, Thomas, 70, 137, 152,
    156
Grenfell, Julian, 147
Gross, John, 45, 49, 51, 52–53,
    61, 65
Grove, George, 51
Guardian, 7
Gulbenkian, Calouste, 125

H———, Captain, 138
Hallam, Arthur Henry, 87
Händel, Georg Friedrich, 130
Hardy, Thomas, 162, 191
Harper's and Queen, 105
Hartley, George, 91
Hawkins, Coleman, 192
Hawthorne, Nathaniel, 76
Haydn, Franz Joseph, 23, 118
Hazlitt, William, 45
Heath, Edward, 99
Heber, Reginald, 155
Henley, William Ernest, 148

Herbert, George, 152
Herrick, Robert, 87, 169
Hitchcock, Alfred, 76
Hoare, Prince, 148
Hodges, Johnny, 192
Hoggart, Richard, 75
Holroyd, Michael, 47
Hopkins, Gerard Manley, 28, 30,
    157, 160
Housman, A. E., 25, 32, 39, 84,
    87, 131, 150, 153, 157, 158,
    161, 162, 183
Howard, Elizabeth Jane, 122
Howe, Julia Ward, 149
Hughes, Ted, 160
Hulme, T. E., 67, 154

Illustrated London News, 17, 105,
    110
Isherwood, Christopher, 42, 144

James, Clive, 167–68, 179
James, Henry, 54, 84
Jesus, 59, 79–80, 178–79
Johnson, Paul, 52–53
Johnson, Samuel, 18, 31, 45, 70,
    83, 152, 156
Jones, Daniel, 71–72
Jonson, Ben, 61
Joyce, James, 82, 193

Keats, John, 21, 70–71, 152
Kelly, Hugh, 156
Kennedy, John F., 59
Kenner, Hugh, 82–83
Kilmarnock, Lady, *see* Bardwell,
    Hilary

202